deaf DUMB blind & STUPID

Book 2

tremayne moore

DEAF, DUMB, BLIND & STUPID (BOOK 2)

A Generational Fight For Life

TREMAYNE MOORE

ISBN Number: 979-8-9908073-6-5 (Paperback)
ISBN Number: 979-8-9908073-5-8 (eBook)
LCC Number: 2026908300

Deaf, Dumb, Blind & Stupid (Book 2): A Generational Fight For Life

Edited by Shantae A. Charles for God Ideas, LLC
Edited by Cynthia M. Portalatin
Cover design by Vonn Media Group, LLC

Published by Maynetre Manuscripts, LLC
PO Box 1819, Owings Mills, MD 21117
www.maynetre.com
Writing To Right The Broken Soul

The author makes no apology for how the very ***REAL*** presence of God in this work of fiction may impact the reader's spiritual life.

Printed in the United States of America
First Printing 2026
10 9 8 7 6 5 4 3 2 1

TABLE OF CONTENTS

ADVANCED PRAISE

Dark, emotional, and unapologetically real, this story explores the scars we carry and the strength it takes to survive them. Tremayne Moore delivers a powerful, faith-centered narrative that challenges, heals, and forces us to feel every moment.

— SHELIA M. GOSS, NATIONAL BESTSELLING AUTHOR OF THE JONESES, DELILAH, AND THE WOMEN IN HOLLYWOOD COLLECTION

Having spent many years helping people navigate the theological claims and cultural pressures of Mormonism, I appreciated Tremayne Moore's willingness to address both spiritual confusion and the painful realities of abuse in this sequel. By bringing difficult subjects into the open, Moore invites readers into an honest conversation about trauma, truth, and the possibility of healing.

— TRACY TENNANT, AUTHOR OF MORMONISM, THE MATRIX, AND ME AND HOST OF THE PODCAST FROM KOLOB TO CALVARY

Tremayne's second book follows the lives of several family members, friends, and the pastor of a young man named Michael Anderson, who—after untold adversities—commits a life-altering decision. Through these survivors' lives, Tremayne examines such delicate and difficult topics as the trauma of abuse, coping and healing, relationships, faith in God, and suicide in a sincere, heartfelt narrative that was so poignant, I had to stop reading at several junctures and just breathe. I have great respect for Tremayne whom I've known since 2011 when he, a Bible believing Christian, contacted me about someone he cared deeply for who was LDS (Mormon).

In 2012, Tremayne's first book, Deaf, Dumb, Blind & Stupid: Michael Anderson's Fight for Life, a fictional memoir from the journal entries of an abused teen, moved me so deeply, I had my university's diversity classes of future teachers read it each semester. Without telling my students ahead of time, Tremayne came and they asked him questions about his life. The book and the experience hearing Tremayne's heart was the highlight of the course for many and Tremayne and I became cherished, yet long-distance, believer friends. I highly recommend both books. Be prepared to experience both heartache and hope.

— DR. LYNN K. WILDER, AUTHOR OF UNVEILING GRACE: THE STORY OF HOW WE FOUND OUR WAY OUT OF THE MORMON CHURCH AND CO-HOST OF THE UNVEILING GRACE PODCAST

CONTENT WARNING

Descriptions of child sexual abuse, emotional abuse, child abuse and suicide ideation. Mature audiences. Readers aged 13-17 may need to be guided through the text.

DEDICATION

As you read this book, you will see and feel my heart through this fictionalized true story. Compared to the first book where the journal entries were solely Michael's, this book is comprised of journal entries by three characters: Stephanie, Carson, and Michael. Stephanie and Carson each have unique fonts to differentiate who's talking.

With that said, I would like to dedicate this book to every victim who's been abused, raped, molested, and to every person that has considered suicide. I also dedicate this book to those who have suffered (or are suffering) from Bipolar Disorder, Post Traumatic Stress Disorder (PTSD), Dissociative Identity Disorder (DID), Borderline Personality Disorder (BPD), Attention Deficit Disorder (ADD), Attention Deficit/Hyperactive Disorder (AD/HD), and to those who are on the spectrum of Autism. Let your voice be heard, even if the world doesn't want to hear it. It's time for the abuser to not be let off the hook. The best way to rectify this is to get the appropriate help you need, not blame yourself for the abuse you suffered, pray, and forgive your abuser. I also add that you need to pray and forgive those who don't want to listen to your voice and who have deafened their ears to your cries for help. Remember Jesus said, "Vengeance is Mine; I will repay." To free yourself is to know the Truth, and the Truth will make you free. We're living in an age where sin is steadily increasing and becoming more tolerable as the love of mankind grows cold. Whatever you do, don't throw your life away, God hasn't forgotten about you. I pray that you read with an open heart and let this book speak to your spirit. You are here with a divine purpose. And last, but definitely not least, I dedicate this book to the children who died before their time.

Parents, if your child or children, tell you they have been abused (or you know one of your children has a mental disorder), you need to take that seriously. I beg you to stop sweeping abuse and mental disorders under the rug, just so you can portray your family as picture perfect. An uninvolved or uninformed parent can be detrimental to the life and health of a child. I encourage you to pray over your children. The enemy seeks to kill, steal and destroy them and our future as a society that cares about the innocent, the weakest and the least of these.

In Loving Memory:

Harry Moore (Father): 1/28/1952 - 9/21/2012

Henry Moore (Uncle): 1/28/1952 - 12/25/2018

Genesis Chalet Rogers: 6/10/1979 - 2/25/2017 (who succumbed to suicide)

DESPITE ...

By Tremayne Moore

Despite the pain, the scars, the abuse, and sorrow
I rise like the eagle, and I spread my wings and fly
I look down below, realizing I overcame the worst
As I soar the heavens, guided by Your Spirit, I can touch the sky.

EXCERPTS FROM BOOK ONE

(For My Newest Readers)

UNHAPPY ENDINGS

Michael's Funeral: 1992

"I know I shouldn't be crying in front of you, but you don't understand how much of a role I played in his life," Bro. Freeman said. "The one thing I wished for Michael was for him to succeed through the trauma he'd faced. I wish I could've stopped him from taking his life. He covered his thoughts of suicide so well, that I couldn't even detect it. He probably would've thought that I would've called him at his home, and his family would've persecuted him for either telling a lie or telling outsiders the family business. I should've read his note right after Sunday school and not waited till after church. I feel partly responsible for his death. I thought counseling was enough. Lord, remove this guilt."

"The enemy has snatched the life of one of your children. I ask, Lord, that we, who are here today, give Michael credit. From my interactions with him, his spirit was so sensitive in that he wanted to ensure that no one was offended, unless it was for a worthy cause. He cared about the hearts of others, and many of us probably overlooked that by saying that he was hypersensitive or melodramatic."

"If we would stop and understand the hearts of others instead of being so judgmental, we could let God minister to our hearts so we could speak life and encouragement to broken and hurting people. I wish Michael would've fallen into the arms of Jesus. He was there with Michael during his hurt and pain. If you've been abused like Michael, He is saying to the little child inside of you, 'I share your pain and they're not just abusing you, they're abusing me. I will repay them, especially if they don't repent.' I said in My Word: 'Woe unto that man by whom the offence cometh. Let me mend your broken heart, and I will bless you double for what you had to endure.'"

"Many people have this question in their mind, especially if they have been a victim of abuse: What happens if the victim dies in the midst of the abuse? This is a valid question. My response is simply this: God would say this to you: Even though their life was short-lived on earth, I promise them a lifetime with Me. Before I close, I'd like for Janice to say a few words, since Michael thought the world of her."

I SPEAK

With tears in my eyes, and guilt in my heart, I find the courage to speak. I know that I am hated by some and pitied by others at this moment, but my care for Michael gives me boldness.

"Thank you, Bro. Freeman. Please forgive me everyone. I feel that I'm at a loss for words. Michael was such a sweetheart, and I know he loved me so much, but I couldn't find an easy way to break his heart. I just abruptly ended our friendship, so I could be with this man who I thought I loved. I didn't realize we had mailed letters to each other on the same day, but this was his letter to me, which I'd like to share with you. I glanced at it the day I received it, but it was like God was telling me to read it that Sunday, and I'm so glad I did:

'Dear Janice: It's hard to live without you when we're in two different states. I know we haven't talked as much since you've been gone. I can only imagine that a long-distance relationship takes a lot of work. I don't know how you feel about it, but I'm committed to it. I know I'm new to relationships, but you know my life story. Please don't hold that against me. But something inside of me tells me that you've found someone to replace me. The thought of that would devastate me. When you kissed me at the airport, you made my heart cry. I literally ran

out of the airport, and I couldn't go to certain places for a few months because every place reminded me of you. I need to be honest with you; saying good-bye is hard for me, especially when two people care about each other. I know we're just friends, but Janice, you mean the world to me. Here's a two-part poem for you entitled "This is Love:"

(Part 1 – Horizontal Version)
I want you for life,
because I'm so in love with you
And thinking of you
is all I want to do
To see birds flying in harmony
is how we're to be
Why are we so divided,
when all we need is unity?
I know you've been gone for a few months,
but it feels like a year
I'm saying this to you
as I'm holding back my tears.
I'm so sorry I couldn't be
what you wanted me to be;
Just know that I love you,
and I still believe in you and me.
Please don't hate me more,
cause I'm pouring my heart to you
The truth is: I see you as He does,
and you are a dream come true.
Honey, I love you,
but you don't care,
I give you my heart,
but your heart's not there.
Maybe I'm crazy
for loving someone like you.
Know that it won't stop
whether or not you love me too
No matter what the world says,

you and I will be restored.
As each day passes,
I realize that I couldn't love you more.
Did you mean what you said
when you said you loved me?
My heart melts and prays
that my dream would be a reality.
Ever since you left me,
I cry as I declare that I miss you
I long for the day that we will be together,
just us two.
As I stare at your picture,
your smile captures my heart,
But I know that the enemy
has captured your soul
to keep us apart.
I don't know what I could say
to make you stay.
Just know you took my heart
the day you walked away.
I'm not giving up on you;
though people are trying to tell me to;
Your soul is too important to me;
I love you just like our Savior loves you.
Whenever I envision your smile,
I would cry when I'm by myself
I know that I just want to be with you
and no one else
I have so much faith in you,
I believe you will be snatched from the fire
You will be set free from the chains;
for it is you that I desire

(Part 2 – Vertical Version)
I know I may not exist
in your eyes

But My love for you
should be no surprise.
You can act holy
and say you love Me
I meant it when I said not to place
another god above Me.
Your heart hates the people
who really love Me
Don't think that a man
will ever rise above Me
You and your friends
are important to Me
No strings are attached with My love;
and yes, it's free.
I know 'till now,
you were naked before My face;
Open your heart to Me,
so, I can clothe you with My grace.
You break My heart
so many times
Trying to avoid Me
with no reason or rhyme.
No matter what you do,
you belong to Me
I knock at the door of your heart
with a promise of eternity
When you wake up,
I am thinking about you
I want you to know Me for who I really am
and of course, to love Me too.
You keep running away from Me,
but I know you can't run forever
You can reject My love,
but I still see us together
You can turn to other gods,
but you are the one I seek for

My love is constantly pouring out to you,
just open your heart's door.
Trust me when I say
I will love you forever
It will be a tragedy
if we don't end up together
Please don't run from My love,
My arms are open wide
Here I stand as your Groom,
hoping you'll be part of My Bride.

I let my tears stream, not caring that makeup was staining my clothes. My heart felt like it was shattering into a thousand pieces, and there was no one who could put me back together.

"Michael was always kind to me, and I led him on at times. I regret doing that now.

He was always encouraging me, and I am actually enjoying the project he wanted me to do. Ever since I read his letter, I wanted to call him, but I didn't get a chance to. I was so busy with my friends for the final three days of his life. But God spoke to me the day of his death, and I started reading the Bible that we had since middle school. The Gospel according to John has opened my eyes so much, and I am starting to understand what it means to be free in Jesus."

"I thought I was in love when I dated my boyfriend, and that he would fill the empty void in me. He couldn't do it; only Jesus was able to. I now know that I don't have to live my life as a second-class citizen, nor believe that my sole purpose in life is to have sex with a man and constantly produce babies in this life and in eternity. It feels so good to know that all I have to do is believe in Jesus and my works are not a part of salvation. I can't believe I'm saying this, but I have never felt so much better in my life."

"Jesus, I repent for how I treated people in the past, and I want You to come into my life, and fill me with Your Spirit. Continue to teach me Your truth and use me for Your glory. I repent and ask those of you who knew Michael to pray for me. I want to be a better friend and be more aware of the needs of others."

I blow a kiss at Michael's coffin. "I'm sorry Michael. I will never forget you."

BRO. FREEMAN CONCLUDES

"I thank you Janice for sharing your story with us. If we don't take suicides and sexual abuse seriously, we're doing ourselves a disservice. There are so many people who are plagued with ADD, ADHD, PTSD, BPD, or are Bipolar, and we steadily punish them for their mental differences and chemical imbalances. Galatians 6:7 says 'Don't be deceived because God is not mocked. Whatever we sow, we will reap.'"

"I ask you a question: Why are we only sympathetic if OUR child has a mental disorder? On the contrary, if you know someone else whose child has a mental disorder, you say 'they need a beating'. This is unfair and reflects the worse part of human nature. If you know someone who is being abused, you need to let them know who to contact if they are being abused, especially when a parent sweeps it under the rug, and they don't want to deal with it. If no one intervenes, the child could very well go on with their life through the abuse and then end up on drugs trying to cure whatever disorder he or she may have."

"And WHY, is nothing done to the parent or the abuser? How do we rectify this problem? Parents, you are to love and protect your children. Once you become a parent, it is no longer about what is convenient for YOU... you are now charged with caring for the life of your child until that child is able to care for him or herself. And one never stops being a parent, even until old age. The greatest gift a parent can give their children is to teach them how to love and to provide a place of nurturing and security; so that they may grow up to fully live out their God-given gifts and in turn share their love with the world."

"If you're a parent, and you've been abused, get help now, and stop sweeping your situation under the rug. This is what brings about generational curses – which you have the power to break – and it also brings about teenage suicide – which is running rampant in this world," Bro. Freeman took a position in front of the pulpit, stepping down in front of Michael's closed casket.

"We as a country are on the brink of losing the next generation. And it's sad that the only remedy for an abused child is drugs or illicit sex. This is one of the many reasons some kids and even adults commit suicide. It's a tragedy that shouldn't happen this way, considering we 'so holy people' are re-victimizing the abused, while the abuser gets away with a crime they should be charged with."

"So, what do we do? Say to the abused, 'the Lord says to forgive and get over it?' That's not an easy fix for someone who has suffered under the hands of the enemy who's trying to kill them. To add insult to injury, no charges are brought up against the abusers who are in some cases even protected by other adults – and cursed is the victim. I'm not saying the victim should go on living life constantly as the victim, but in the midst of the abuse, why curse the victim? Their life is already a living hell to them, and all we're doing is damning them to a hell they might go, especially if they don't know the Lord."

"Somebody needs to hear them, or we as a country will continue to lose God-gifted people to the hands of death. Either abused victims will take their own lives, or they will become sadistic and take somebody else's life. If we don't discern their hearts and pray for them, these are the consequences that teenagers will suffer along with people who are dying. We know this to be true with the increase in cases of mass murder linked to abuse and bullying."

"It's amazing to me, how we treat each other, especially if we say we're Christians. A person who's lost, depressed, or has suffered under the pain of domestic, physical, sexual, or emotional abuse can have a gun to their head, and we have the unmitigated gall to simply say, "I'm sorry," or "I'll pray for you." That's not helping a hurting soul – in fact, you're enabling them. Try coming out of your comfort zone for once and stop being so selfish. Try saying, 'Can we talk about this? I want to listen to you, and you have my undivided attention.' Talk to me somebody! Band-Aids and clichés and prideful statements like, 'I'm the leader,' or 'Come to me with every problem you have' only to make you the poster child or for you to be chastised; though I don't have to share my problems with you unless I reveal what I want, will never heal a serious wound in a person who really needs healing for their mind, body and soul."

"We do need a healing for the soul of mankind, because mankind is full of darkness and death. Let's try giving unselfish love and compassion away. Someone needs it! If we as a church don't want to bear burdens or pray, we are rendering ourselves motionless–together we stand, divided we fall. Love has been lacking in these last days. Yes, some will say it's not their fault; again, it's on them, and they must answer to God for how they treat people."

"Of course, we're human and sinful, but we must die to self daily, because if we continue to focus on what's positive – and not negative, for Jesus did say in this world, we will have tribulation – then we're walking around blind and oblivious to what's going on around us. When we tell children they need to submit to their abuser, keep their mouth shut, and serve God in the process, what message are we sending them?"

"When we lack agape love, our loved ones take their lives, and the world is going to hell first class with the help of those who claim to be the Church. I recommend you take some time out in your life to study what agape love really is. I guarantee you this will change your life."

"Let me declare this: if a Church says Christ or professes to be Christian, and never reads the four gospels, you and that church are shortchanging God. And why do we run from His teachings, if we say we believe in Jesus? Again, talk to me!"

"I beg you today, to consider the words of Matthew 7:21-23: 'Not everyone that says to me, Lord, Lord, shall enter into the kingdom of heaven; but he that does the will of my Father which is in heaven. Many will say to me in that day, Lord, Lord, have we not prophesied in thy name? And in thy name have cast out devils? And in thy name done many wonderful works? And then will I profess unto them, I never knew you: depart from me, ye that work iniquity.' John 6:40 says, and this is Jesus speaking: 'And this is the will of him that sent me, that everyone which sees the Son, and believeth on him, may have everlasting life: and I will raise him up at the last day.'"

"If churches claim that they are THE Church, and no other church is teaching them correctly (except for that respective church), and you have a high number of divorces and suicides, then that church and leader will have an awful lot of explaining to do come judgment time."

"I wonder how many times we go about life not seeking the Truth, because we sometimes feel within ourselves that we have it. If you want to be sure of receiving eternal life and not just hope you receive eternal life, please see me after this service."

"Victims of any form of abuse need to know they are loved, especially if they've been abused as a child. No one is telling them that they're loved, and we, as a society are punishing them; no one is bringing out their God-given talents. Jesus loves even the abuser, and calls him or her to repent, and yes, He loves the abused. He wants to heal the abused, and He does so with love. If we're calling ourselves Christians, we need to LOVE them. The truth is that we don't love them; we're punishing them, just because they don't meet our fleshly standards. We're killing them with our words, and this is why many abused people are leaning towards suicide. Yes, we're not perfect, but we've got to do better."

"If you have been abused, regardless of what type it is, I know you probably feel that you don't fit into society, and no one hears your voice. You have many questions in your mind, such as, "Why did God allow this to happen to me? I thought He loved me?" It's a mystery that we'll never understand. Part of me believes that you went through what you did; not because He doesn't love you, but you are the person who will be able to encourage and motivate someone else who has been abused to go forward with their life. The other reason is that we live in a fallen world, and we are suffering the effects of sin, which brings on every evil work."

"Even though Michael is no longer with us physically, I'm sure he wanted us to hear his message. I know we're living in a time where love is cold. And how we treat you isn't right. It's bad enough that the world doesn't want to hear you, and it's more devastating when the church doesn't want to hear you. No one is available to be a sounding board to you, but let me say that Jesus is always listening, and He will be your sounding board. I know it hurts when people feel that you're taking up their space, and that you have to be perfect like them. I stand guilty at times, and I'll be honest with you, this is where the church gets a black eye."

"We need to stop letting the devil gain access to your brain, or our selfishness will never allow you to get freedom. We have to stand beside each other as brothers and sisters in the Lord. We are all God's children, and we can't carry on like its business as usual. As Christians, we ARE to be our 'brother's keepers,' and to do so in a spirit of love."

"Let me also say this: your first step to freedom is to forgive all the parties involved. This includes those who abused you and those who turned a blind eye to the situation: if you feel you can't approach them, turn them over to the Lord. I know you're thinking that they are getting a pass for what they did, according to the world. I promise you, if they don't repent and change their ways, they will pay for their sins."

"The devil tried to kill you, but you're still alive. Take the life you still have, and give the devil a black eye by loving God with your heart and fulfilling His will for your life. You have a powerful testimony, and don't let the dark cloud of your past hinder your future. I love you, and there are people here who are ready to hug and embrace you."

"I need to add there will be some people in the world and in the church who are selfish, who think they're better than you, because they didn't have to experience what you did and will ridicule you for what you had to endure. Simply remove them from your life, because they don't care about you and are just being used by the devil. Make a stand for the sake of this and future generations. It's time that a blind eye be opened to Jesus, the Light of the World."

"We cannot continue to live in darkness. Why are we so nonchalant over things that break God's heart? How can we adults sit and scoff at them when they are victims of heinous crimes, bullying, and mental abuse by simply telling them to 'get over it?' Yet, they take their lives and we still scoff at them? Be thankful for the life God has given you, please!"

BRO. FREEMAN'S WARNING

"I want to talk to the abusers, because I know they come to church too: you may think you're getting away with the crime you're committing and putting your demonic spirit onto these victims, causing them to be on medications and counseling, as they try to rediscover who they really are while possibly standing on the brink of suicide. In this world, you might actually be getting away with it, but remember, God knows exactly what you have done. If you don't repent from your HEART, not just saying 'I'm sorry for getting caught,' then eternal judgment from God awaits you."

"If you don't take anything away from this funeral, I pray you take this away: everyone will bow down to the True and Living God; this includes angels and those who claim to be a god. The Scripture says that God humbles the exalted, and He exalts the humble. Michael's life was not in vain. I hope his fight for life will stir you to fight for your own life. Fight for the lives of your children. Fight for justice for the abused. Fight for the right of your children to enjoy their childhood and not have their innocence stripped from them. I encourage you, friends, saints, and even those merely here to witness a burial, to fight for life. Yes, if there was nothing else Michael did, he fought hard. He wins if he changed your mind today."

PROLOGUE

Immediately After The Funeral

Brother Freeman concluded the funeral and he turned Michael's journal over to Viola, Michael's mother. Once she received it, she immediately ran out of the sanctuary and into the foyer. Gerald, Michael's father, ran after her to determine what was going on. He thought that she must be crushed and sorrowful for the fact that Michael is gone from us and too soon. While the rest of the family and friends sat in the sanctuary, it was evident there was a bit of a scuffle taking place in the foyer, as shouts, raised voices and the distinct words of blame-shifting went on. Stephanie, Michael's sister, who had been sitting in the sanctuary for a few minutes, could not resist going out to the foyer to see what was causing the commotion.

Gerald was pacing back and forth, while Viola stood stoic with a look of disbelief on her face.

"Are you okay?" Gerald asks.

"I'm fine," Viola responded. "I can't believe that Michael lied about me and said all he did. I'm not responsible for his death!"

Gerald, shocked, shouted at Viola: "*You* killed our son!"

"I did no such thing! That was his choice to end his life! And how dare you stick up for him! You're supposed to stick up for me!" Viola shouted back, her hands clenched tightly by her sides, her face wearing rage, no longer stoic.

"How *dare* you?" Gerald looked at her incredulously. "You are a *complete* narcissist! You probably don't even remember saying that you never wanted a son the day he died. Oh, about me sticking up for you. That's my obligation; however, this is different. We had an obligation to protect Michael."

Viola, still in rage mode, blurted, "You can speak for yourself. I was a good mother to Michael!"

Gerald had enough, and said, "You need to just be for real. I believe Teddy P gave a dissertation on that!"

With that, Viola lunged at Gerald in an attempt to unleash her rage on him. But before Viola could fully engage, Stephanie, who'd had enough, blocked her as if she were a defensive linebacker. After gaining control of her mom, Stephanie's voice overruled them.

"STOP IT! Whether you want to believe this or not, Michael is dead!" Stephanie thundered, as her voice trembled with frustration.

Heeding Stephanie's words, Gerald and Viola gathered their belongings, head down, and walked out of the church. Stephanie's cry from the foyer was so loud, it stirred Janice to come out of the sanctuary to comfort Stephanie, who overcome by grief, was crying uncontrollably.

"I want to keep in touch with you," Janice Baker, Michael's friend, whispered in Stephanie's ear as she hugged her. "There are some things I want you to know about Michael that you will want to keep in mind when raising your soon-to-be-born child," Janice shared.

"Here's my phone number. Please call me soon; so, I can get your number and write it in my address book. Also, in the event my phone number changes, I can update you."

"Thank you, that would mean a lot," Stephanie replied, nodding as she hugged Janice.

GOOD AFTERNOON, DIARY

33 Years Later

Good afternoon, Diary. This is Stephanie Anderson, and I'm sitting here writing my thoughts down. I say, it's better to write it now; so, I don't forget. Plus, I want to leave a legacy to my son, his wife and his expected children. Wow, it seems like a lifetime ago. I am now in my 50s, and it seems like time does fly when you're having fun living this thing called life. My life has had some up days, and I surely have seen some down days. I will admit that I was the spoiled child to my parents, and I had the attitude that you couldn't tell me anything. I guess the apple surely didn't fall far from the tree; I am the spitting image of my mother. I don't know if that's a good thing or a bad thing.

Here I am with a son in his 30s. Initially, he didn't grow me up, considering I was still young, and I did some things that I was not proud of. I would say, life was going to take me out if I didn't change my ways. Although I was able to graduate from Howard University with my degree in psychology. Eventually, my pastor taught me the concept of change that would shake me to the core. When he prayed over me, he spoke these words: "If you don't change, your life will be cut short." That was a hard decision I had to face; yet, I knew I had to make the hard decision to change. I knew that if I didn't change, I could not be sure of what life my son would have. Granted, I could've been the mama that the late rapper 2Pac mentioned in "Dear Mama." I would say that my late father kept me sane enough to not go down that route.

In the midst of it all, I had it good. And not to gloat, it was better than my brother's life, who is gone from us. Thinking back, I didn't like Michael. I was jealous of him when he really was jealous of me. My parents spoiled me so much that I thought I had the best life. Since he's been gone, I've had the time and space to reflect. Now, I understand why he felt the way he felt. I kind of regret not being the little sister that he needed me to be.

At the time, my world was about me. I was just taking after my mother, as it's all about her in her world. Maybe, I'm going through a mid-life crisis, and I just need to get all these thoughts out of my mind and on to some paper. Maybe it's menopause. Truth be told, I should've known something was wrong the night before Michael took his life. He played Michael Bolton's "How Am I Supposed To Live Without You" and Alfie Silas' "There I Go" so many times that I was threatening to take his cassette from him and break it. He would not stop crying when listening to both songs, nor did I bother to check on him, as I was dealing with pregnancy at the time. I could imagine for Michael, his life was flashing before him with the abuse and rejection that he endured when listening to those two songs.

During this time, I remember my mother saying to Michael that he wasn't fit for college and that he was to live at home. Back then, I was happy that our parents allowed me to do whatever I wanted to do, and that I wasn't blamed for my wrongs, even though Michael was blamed for what he did and what he didn't do. It was like he couldn't win for nothing. I made a mental note to myself back then to not do to my son Carson what my mother did to Michael. I saw so much greatness in Carson during his youth, and now, he's a full-grown man, about to walk into his destiny.

I think back to that dreadful day, sitting in Severna Community Church, hearing Brother Elliot Freeman. Wow. At the time, that's how I saw it. Now, I see it as an eye-opener. It seems like yesterday when all this transpired, just as it seems like it was yesterday when Carson was born. May of 1993 changed my life. I had just turned 17 years old when I gave birth to Carson.

Janice has kept her promise to me, and we still keep in touch—though not as much now due to some health challenges, but I know Janice is doing well with her life. I wish I could say more, but wait, let me grab Carson's journal. He just gave it to me as he is now getting married. Let me also grab Michael's journal and place it next to Carson's. I don't know what to expect, after all that I've experienced during my teen years and my 20s. This generation today concerns me, and I pray against the spirits of apathy, entitlement and disrespect that I see in so many of our youth.

I encouraged Carson to start writing when he was 10 years old, because that was around the time Michael started his journal. I did everything I could to let my son have his privacy and still be his mother, even though Viola was determined to disrupt our privacy as children. If anything, I ensured Carson's safety, and yeah, you could call me overprotective, especially after what had happened to Michael. Maybe that was why I was hard on Carson from the start, until I had a rude awakening that I was acting too much like my mother. I could only imagine what he would write about me during those times. Thankfully, I was able to apologize for many of the whippings that he didn't deserve. Truthfully, Michael didn't deserve much of his frequent whippings either; there were times I thought he would just get one for waking up.

I managed to get Michael's journal after my father

passed away. That was a hard death to take, about as bad as Michael's death. I thought I was the special child based on how my parents treated me, and to a degree, I still am. I'm surprised my parent's marriage survived after Michael's death, and truthfully, how both of my parents were able to sleep at night, knowing that Michael was no longer there. We would never hear him nor see him again. Michael sure loved him some Janice, and Janice's speech had me crying. Sadly, Viola was just being her normal self. I must admit, there was a part of me that was glad he was gone as it solidified that it was all about me. Gerald was angry to the point that, if looks could kill, he would have hurt the next person who got in his way.

And while I'm on the subject of people passing away, let me talk about my father Gerald. After the funeral and the numerous arguments, Gerald became increasingly addicted to smoking and drinking, nonstop. Even though he didn't drink as much whiskey, he couldn't lay off the rum. And even though he stopped snorting cocaine and smoking marijuana, he couldn't stop smoking cigarettes altogether. My mom, Viola, didn't make matters any better. It seemed like the abuse that she previously dished out to Michael now had a new target: my father. To be frank, living under these conditions would have made anybody drink as an escape route. Thankfully, I don't drink. Seeing what it did to my father was enough to not make me go down that road. I'm surprised Michael didn't even take up drugs as a way of escape, even though tragically, Michael's mental anguish drove him to suicide.

Now, let me take a deep breath because my tears threaten to blur these words. It's like suicide was a permanent fix to a temporary situation. If he could've kept his head up, he would've made it out of the house. Then again, the control my mom had over him might have made it impossible. It was like she treated him like he was nothing, the son she never wanted. To my mom, what my father or Michael did was never good enough for her. She expected perfection out of them, and when she didn't get it, hell had no fury!

Unfortunately, with Gerald, everything came to a halt when he came down with lung cancer and emphysema that progressed rapidly. The doctors quickly gave up on him and left him to die. I'll be honest; I didn't want to see him suffer. With that diagnosis came multiple medicines that my mother and I had to administer and monitor, and it was difficult, especially with him sleeping constantly. Bathing him was disheartening. After a slow deterioration, he would pass away years later. His funeral was heartfelt, and I saw people I hadn't seen in years. I knew my life would never be the same with him gone. I can say this; I'm thankful I had him for as long as I did. Not too many women in my age group knew their fathers, or as the adage goes, "their fathers were rolling stones."

Despite the deeds he did, he taught me what to

expect in a man. And granted, there were times I didn't listen. Now that I'm older, and having a great pastor as a father figure, I'm understanding about what it means to have integrity below my waist. Do I know if I'm going to be married again? Only time will tell. I will say that I'm so happy for my son. He's experienced so much, and it's so sad that my mom and I don't even talk any more. Maybe, one day, we'll be able to reconcile and put our differences aside. Maybe, I need to listen to my pastor's words on agape and honor, until I can let it get into my heart and spirit. I'm open to reconciliation, but that takes both sides wanting to make it happen.

After my father passed, I felt I had to read Michael's journal, as it just seemed like the home environment that I grew up in was just hell on earth. Once I read it, I was able to see a lot of what my son Carson had to go through. I'll admit, my ego subsided as I witnessed Carson go through a lot of similar things. Well, let me read Carson's journal and then, as I thumb through his pages, write in my journal. I know Carson loves me, and I'm so glad he gave me permission to share with you all; so, others won't have to feel alone in their pain, and hopefully, they won't have to take their lives or injure themselves to escape whatever pain they're going through.

I remember when Carson was born, It was May 3, 1993. It was like God smiled on me when He gave me my son. My parents adored him, and my father ensured that he would take care of me, since my baby daddy didn't want to have anything to do with him. As I watched Carson grow, I could imagine how Michael grew up. I see similarities between my son and my brother; so, that gave me a keen awareness of what to watch for.

Michael was very gifted. I remember what he wrote in his journal in late 1988, and now I laugh at it. This is what it says:

Michael's Journal
December 6, 1988:

I don't feel like hearing the radio now. All I hear is either "Superwoman" by Karyn White or "Thanks for My Child" by Cheryl 'Pepsii' Riley. I actually like Superwoman; however, I hate "Thanks For My Child." Why? This is just an anthem for single mothers to show that they don't need a man in their lives after they have a child. Yet, they will turn around and call him a deadbeat. The question I would ask is "Why did you choose him in the first place?"

Present Day:

When I read that, I thought, he had a gift to see into the future. If Michael were here, he would probably detest "Waiting To Exhale" and hate Savannah's character and especially Robin's character. Michael wanted to be the perfect gentleman, yet the women chose deadbeats and then turned around and complained about them. Granted, I loved the movie, as I could easily relate. Carson hasn't seen the movie, but he would probably agree with Michael. People like Carson and Michael are able to see things that an average person can't see. Some call it pattern recognition. In short, Michael was definitely ahead of his time. I remember when I was pregnant, I was playing "Thanks For My Child" heavily! And Michael really didn't like me, because I was getting so much attention. His jealousy over me, his heartbreak over Janice, and how people treated him just took him over the edge.

Before I start going through Carson's journal, I must make it known that I was going through post-partum depression after my pregnancy, which lasted a few years. The doctor also wanted me to see a counselor, and the counselor diagnosed me as bipolar based on my home environment and several other factors. One thing I made sure of was that I took my medication and prayed in faith that I was healed. I wanted to be the one to show that this illness wasn't "just in my mind," nor that I was believing for my healing yet not participating in the healing aspect that medicine brought.

I believe I covered my late father and a little bit about Janice, but I don't believe I mentioned my mother. I'll cover her as I read Carson's journal. Brother Freeman is my mentor as he was a big brother to Michael. Every now and then, I talk to him and he's helped me a lot in this journey through life. Brother Freeman is such a gentleman, and he loves Carson as if he were Brother Freeman's son. See, every man needs to have a man covering him - as men should be each other's brother's keeper. In fact, I remember Brother Freeman said that the strength of a nation is determined by its male population. So, what is Brother Freeman doing now?

He's nearing completion of a sanctuary for abused victims. He's so into protecting children from the harms of the devil, as my son is too!

CARSON'S EARLY CHILDHOOD

I am smiling in anticipation as I open Carson's journal to read his words:

July 15, 2003:

My mom loves me. She bought me this book for me to write in. I just turned 10 years old, and she is the greatest woman on this earth. Mommy knows I struggle in writing because I'm vernally behind in school.

July 17, 2003:

I overhear my mom and Nanna arguing. Mommy is telling Nanna to keep it down because I can hear. Nanna still shouts and says to Mommy that I'm slow. Why does Nanna think that?

August 12, 2003:

Mommy and I went school shopping and she bought me what I wanted for school: a Trapper Keeper!

September 2, 2003:

I'm start the 5th grade, and I like my teachers. Some of my friends from the fourth grade are in my class, yet one of my friends was held back.

September 9, 2003:

Mommy told me to tell her if someone tries to harm me and that she loves and will protect me.

October 10, 2003:

I had deetenshun at school, and I got a whippin when I came home. All I did was call out twice. Sometimes I feel I can't help myself.

October 25, 2003:

I got another whippin because I didn't fold the clothes correctly. I got whippins when I was younger, too. But now, they hurt more.

November 12, 2003:

I accidentally let out a cussword (after hearing Papa say

one), and my mom smacked me in my face! This smack left a bruise on the right side of my face!

December 25, 2003:

Christmas is my favorite holiday! My grandmother came over, and she brought Uncle Woody over so he could meet me. I could hear my mom and my grandma arguing about Uncle Woody because mom didn't want Uncle Woody over our house. He shouted that there is no Santa Claus! No Santa?!

June 14, 2004:

My mom put me in a summer program, and my Uncle Woody dropped by to bring me some candy.

August 15, 2004:

Grandma came to our house and brought Uncle Woody over. He asked if I wanted to go to the store with him. I can get some candy if I go. Grandma was eager for me to go, that way she can talk to Mom. Uncle Woody took me to the store and when we parked the car, he forced me into the backseat. He told me to not say a word, or he would shoot me with the gun that's inside his glove compartment. He was hurting me with his body parts. I can't tell my mom what happened because he told me not to tell her. I am afraid of what he might do.

September 6, 2004:

I'm starting the 6th grade, and I'm so excited. I'm one year away from being a middle school student.

September 7, 2004:

First day of school was great; however, I had to go to Uncle Woody's house before I went home. While I was over there, he was watching a movie while touching himself. I'm thinking to myself, what is he doing? Before I could see what was on TV, he locks me in another room. I was in there for about an hour or so, and he asked me if I wanted to get out and watch TV. Once I said yes, he started wiggling his torso, and that was telling me he wanted to hurt me again. I don't like it, nor do I like him! How will I be able to tell my mom and she believe me? Uncle Woody made it clear that if I told, no one, including my mom, would believe me. Before I left the room, he asked me who my daddy was. I had to lie and say he was, in order for him to let me out. I am afraid of what Uncle Woody will do.

Present Day:

I feel so bad that I left Carson with Uncle Woody. I wasn't thinking about Carson at the time, I was simply trying to make a living for my son and me. Maybe I was thinking that Michael was an isolated victim. Woody should've been registered as a sex offender; yet, I'm sure that my mom would've fought to not let that happen.

I remember when my brother was getting whippings from my mom because she believed he was lying about Uncle Woody. Looking back, he didn't deserve any whipping at all, knowing what I know now about what he did to my son. The truth is that my mom was throwing my brother to the wolves, as if he didn't matter to her. Okay. Back to Carson's Journal.

April 14, 2005:

Uncle Woody took me to school, and I hate him. All he did on the way to school, was cuss at me and tell me that I was a faggot and that no one would believe me if I told on him. They were right, they both believed Uncle Woody and I was grounded for a week. I couldn't go outside or play my game!

April 15, 2005:

Mommy took me to the doctor because I wasn't feeling good and it was painful to go to the bathroom. The nurse came out and said somebody was touching me and that whoever touched me harmed me. My mommy screamed in anger and then called my grandma. My grandma was blaming me and my mommy for the pain. I told my mommy that Uncle Woody touched me. The nurse told my mommy to call the police and she did. My grandma told her not to, but my mommy did it anyway. I heard my grandma say that I was lying, which is not true. I don't trust my grandma.

Present Day:

I remember that day so well. And to think my mom had the nerve to take Uncle Woody's side! Thankfully, I was able to catch myself, and I too almost took Uncle Woody's side, as he was older. I guess it's just natural to believe the adult and not the child, if there is a difference of opinion. The more I think about it, that's the same Uncle that was molesting Michael, and my mother did everything she could to protect him. I know Michael envied me because I was getting all the attention, but now I am starting to understand the why. It was almost like she was sending the message that all she cared about was herself. Now, I see it as a cry for love, a love that my mother never received. That's actually why we don't talk.

I'm a little heartbroken that Carson didn't come to me when it first happened. But I understand when a child is scared and threatened with such malice that the magnitude of the moment must have been terrifying. A child is going to do everything possible to save his own life and protect those he loves, and really, self-preservation is normal. Granted, people today are dying by the dozens because of abuse, drug addiction and reckless behavior. Many of them are not even living past 18, and some are dying younger than that. It breaks my heart to hear that; yet, I'm thankful that I'm still alive and my son is about to do great things and make his mark in the world.

Oh, you know; it's funny that Michael and I grew up with the philosophy of, "what goes on in the house, stays in the house." I had to break that mindset for Carson, because I could only imagine what he would have done, if he had kept all of that inside of him. I'm sure if Michael weren't suffering from a mental illness, he would probably have been sent to jail for having murdered Uncle Woody. I believe his mental illness saved him from doing that.

Okay, let me continue reading. I do tend to go off on tangents at times. Wait, I think this entry is important, because I remember wanting Carson to talk to Brother Freeman.

THE MEETING

June 15, 2008:

My mom wanted me to talk to Brother Freeman about what happened to me with Uncle Woody. Brother Freeman told me that I endured the same thing that my Uncle Michael experienced. Sadly, he left this earth too soon. He told me that Michael had so many questions for him. He felt his pain when he asked. His death has caused Brother Freeman to create a sanctuary for people who have experienced what Michael and I went through.

He said to me: "There's a part of me that failed your late Uncle by not speaking up when I should have. He had a calling of God on his life that no one will get to experience. But I have dedicated a part of my life to being an advocate for people like you and your late Uncle. There are so many people who have stopped pursuing destiny because of their trauma, and people are hurt by church members' lack of empathy. Members of the church that Michael attended did him wrong and many didn't care if he lived or died. That should never be the attitude we have."

"One of Michael's cries was that it seemed like those who did wrong got better treatment from God than those who had been victimized. What I say to you is this, God is not like us mere humans. We have a tendency to take the side of the relative more than we do the child. Sadly, your grandmother took the side of your relative and not you, the grandchild. All you can do is pray for her and love her. I think it's best that you talk to your mom and do all that you can to stay away from Uncle Woody."

"I will say this to you, and I remember saying this to your late Uncle before he passed: We must have faith in our Creator to know that He has ordered our steps, and He knows you've been wronged. You don't have the mental capacity to process this right now, because you are still growing. I also need to correct something I said to Michael that I will now say to you. Initially, I said that I was thankful to God for everything, the good and the bad. But I have matured in my life to now where I realize that I'm thankful in all things and not for all things, as God did not orchestrate the bad in my life. I don't know if you've ever read a children's Bible. That's a great place to start for you. The book of Job shows the conversation between God and the devil. The devil did everything he could to get Job to curse God, yet he didn't. God wasn't behind the evil that was done to Job. It was the devil. I want you to see that God wasn't behind the evil that was done to you. It was the devil."

I asked Brother Freeman if Uncle Woody is a demon. He said that was a little harsh, but that Uncle Woody has a spirit inside of him that's not of God at all.

Present Day:

Wow, I would say that Uncle Woody is possessed with a demon for the mere fact that if you are harming innocent children, that's a spirit designed to steal, kill and destroy. I had to jump ahead for a minute; so, let me go back to when Carson faced his brush with school faculty.

September 9, 2005:

I was suspended from school because a classmate touched me on my shoulder, out of nowhere, and I punched him in his face.

Present Day:

I remember that day, and now that I think about it, Uncle Woody did some psychological damage to his mind! I now understand that Carson had been traumatized and triggered by what seemed like an innocent touch. I had to explain to the faculty what was going on in my family, after which my mom wouldn't talk to me for a couple of days. She called my son a liar! However, after testing, I was made aware that my son had special needs. Wait, after reading about Carson's suspension, I realized Michael was definitely a special needs child. God's timing was perfect. At that time, I was going to call Brother Freeman, but he actually called to check on me. So, I was able to fill him in on what happened to

Carson. He said he wasn't surprised, considering what Uncle Woody did to Michael. When he said that, I thought about the mentioning of knives and Uncle Woody stabbing him.

September 12, 2005:

My mom talked to Brother Freeman, and he encouraged my mom to sign me up for a therapy support group. I feel okay about it, and I'll see what happens.

October 1, 2005:

I found out that I was transferred to an alternative school because of my suspension. I am happy that it won't be permanent. If I can prove to them that I can control my emotions, then I can go back to my normal school.

Present Day:

Why did people have to say, "normal school?" That's the problem today; we must classify everything. In some areas, it's discrimination and viewed as labelling children. It's not fair. Culture does not have the right to label my child, or any child for that matter.

THE SUPPORT GROUP

October 15, 2005:

This was my first day at the support group. They call it Cognitive Behavioral Intervention for Trauma in School (CBITS). It's therapy for coping with trauma and to reduce post-traumatic stress disorder (PTSD). There were about four boys in the group, including me, and there were about six girls in the group. Most of the boys in the group had similar stories like mine and we were diagnosed with PTSD. Two of the girls in our group were told they had dissociative identity disorder (DID). The facilitator told us that DID usually comes when a child, who is around five-years-old, is abused or raped.

What I like about this group is that we are all in middle school and we go to the same school. I would see them in the hallways but never knew them. One of the girls was sold by her drug-addict mother to men for sex at the age of five.

Another girl was sexually assaulted when she was five; who was a member of the clergy. He would tell her she was attractive, even at that age. She said it started as a hug, and then she would end up in pain after being with him.

The facilitator, though trained, was still in shock, and couldn't believe what he was hearing. He went to seek help as to what he could do for the two girls who had spoken about their sexual abusers. Sadly, he couldn't do anything because the parents believed the girls were making this up.

When the facilitator came back to the meeting, he was not happy. Under his breath, he said: "These girls are being trafficked and there's nothing I can do about it." I asked him what he meant by that. He said he'd try to explain as simple as possible: "This is where someone is sold to people, to traffic them. Basically, make someone nothing more than a sex object." I asked what can happen to a person. He said, many things could happen. Apart from physical damage to a person's body, there's psychological damage to a person's soul and spirit. He also said many people who are placed in this situation have done bodily harm to themselves such as cutting, burning parts of their skin, and even worse, some have contemplated or even attempted suicide.

I asked the facilitator if he believed I was trafficked. He asked me, if my perpetrator had passed me off to other people for sexual activity. I said no; so, he said I wasn't trafficked.

October 15, 2005 (later that evening):

I asked my mom if I was trafficked. She said, "No; however, she believed my late uncle was after having read his journal. She said my uncle was passed off to other people by

Uncle Woody for his enjoyment; so, I would say that he was trafficked.

Present Day:

I remember this conversation with Carson, and I had to call Brother Freeman about this, because that could've easily been me, if I were to have switched places with Michael. Uncle Woody put Michael through hell, and my mom was of no help. I mentioned the two girls Carson spoke to me about to Brother Freeman, and he sighed before saying:

"This is definitely a work of the devil - and some people would call it a ritual abuse, for the fact that the person who is destroying these kids' lives is possessed by the devil with the aim of destroying not only their innocence but also is after their souls to ultimately destroy their souls. Some of these kids never make it out of it alive, or they are alive physically, yet they are dead mentally, spiritually and emotionally. Now, would I call it that? I don't know; however, I would say that it's an attack on our youth from the very ones who gave them life. What is heartbreaking for me is that when people in the church are doing the abusing, or using the cloth to do the abuse, they are going to cause the victims to not want to have anything to do with church. Even worse, they will more and likely punish God for something He had no part in."

November 2, 2005:

I finally know the girls' names: the girl who was sold at five is Genobia Rogers and the girl who was raped by her father is Melissa Stone.

December 6, 2005:

Our counseling session met again. We discussed self-harm, and the girls who were diagnosed with DID say that they both self-harm. How do they hide it from others? Surely, a doctor would know if they had a physical done.

March 8, 2006:

My mom shared with me a page from Michael's journal. She wanted me to know what her father said about our sexual organs. I believe it was when Michael was about 11 years old. She said that her father told Michael that God made a penis for a man and a vagina for a woman. So, I asked my mom if what Uncle Woody did to me was natural. She said no. I asked what Papa would say. She said he would adamantly say it's not natural. Mom said to me that we are uniquely gifted and we are the sex that we are supposed to be. She encouraged me to embrace my manhood, as she embraced her womanhood.

Present Day:

Michael wrote in his journal that when he was 11-years-old learning about sexual intercourse in school, he was trying to understand how Marvin Gaye's song "Sexual Healing" fit in the equation.

I laughed at that, because we didn't know what we were singing at the time, but now I know what it means. If he was here, he would be much older and would be able to answer that question on his own.

SPECIAL NEEDS

September 12, 2006:

I'm glad I have some men in my life from church who serve as guides. They are teaching me what it means to be a young man and not a boy, and that there is no shame in loving God. They expect us to respect our elders, and to treat people with the utmost respect. If only adults would do the same.

I met this blond-haired girl named Jennifer Grey at my middle school. The way her hair waved at me just caused me to stare. I felt somewhat self-conscious because my skin is breaking out due to this acne thing, but I decided to talk to her. It was pouring rain outside, and she didn't have an umbrella as we were leaving school for the day. So, I walked her to her parents' car using my umbrella to cover her, and she just smiled at me as she got in the car. My heart almost leaped out of me when she smiled. Could this be the beginning of something?

September 13, 2006:

I saw Jennifer at lunch today, and I was happy that she was by herself. I asked her if I could sit with her and she allowed me to. Just the conversation we had kept me on a cloud for the rest of the day. I was given a book by her today, and it was a blue book, known as the Book of Mormon. I brought it home with me, and my mom asked me what I was reading. She started to snatch the book away from me, but then she suddenly stopped and left the room. I'm not sure why.

Present Day

I nodded my head when I read that part. I almost went into a "Viola moment" that day, and I had to catch myself. I remembered how my mom had chewed Michael out for the same thing. In fact, I can still hear her words loud and clear: "You're not Mormon! They are racists, and no Blacks attend their church!" I caught myself, and decided to let him read it for now, but later, I called Brother Freeman about it, so, he could prepare his talk with Carson. I made sure that Carson was more focused on his Children's Bible if he was going to hold onto the Book of Mormon.

As I was reading Michael's journal, I realized he had some questions about the groups of people who are in the Book of Mormon. He had asked Janice about it, but she didn't know, and dismissed the questions. So, when Jennifer gave Carson that book, I asked him if he knew who the people in the book were, and he said no. He took the book to school and asked a history teacher if they existed, and they didn't say. He then asked Jennifer, and she dismissed his question just like Janice did with Michael.

You know, when I was about 11, I remember Michael did something which, in my mom's eyes, was embarrassing to her. Little did she know, I watched with a smile when she smacked Michael in the face for his offense. One thing Michael used to do was make all kinds of faces.

Now that I am older, I can see that there were times that he did not know what he was doing. So, why am I mentioning this? I recall my studies at Howard University, and having dealt with so many children, I now realize that Michael was most likely undiagnosed autistic. And my mother chastised him so much for being so different. The more I think about it, this was the main reason so many girls did not like him. He was different, and to him, a girlfriend was everything. It kept his father off his back, not wondering if he was gay, or if he was even thinking about sex at all. As I read his journal, it was evident that he loved God and had such a heart for Him. I feel bad for not only how I treated him, but also the role I played in his death. Thankfully, it was nowhere near as heavy as the role that my parents played in it, Yet I must be accountable for my part, regardless of how great or small it was.

I had mentioned girlfriends just a moment ago, but

I remember an entry that Michael wrote in 1990 about the talent show, and how he broke down and cried during a song he sang.

Michael's Journal
March 30, 1990:

It is talent show night again. This time I sang Michael Bolton's "How Am I Supposed to Live Without You." Of course, I announced that this was dedicated to someone in the audience. I'm sure everyone in the audience knew it was for Janice. I barely survived the second verse, because tears were flowing down my cheek. I got through it, and Janice gave me a hug.

Present Day

I admit, his love for music really helped me through some difficult situations. In fact, I created some You Tube playlists with songs that he mentioned from his journal. Sometimes, I even fall asleep listening to them. Compared to the music today, the music he loved is soothing. I know; I am rambling. So, let me stay on task with what I really want to write about.

The more I thought about Michael, I realized that I had to get Carson evaluated and assessed for autism back in 2008. I know; I should have had that done when he was in elementary school. But you know; my mom and I got into an argument about this concept of Autism. She now believes Carson is on the spectrum, but she sure didn't believe it back then along with Michael being on the spectrum. It was around this time when celebrities were sounding the alarm. I initially did not think anything about it until CNN did a documentary on it, and I realized that Carson and Michael had exhibited the characteristics of autism. I remember Michael being placed on Ritalin, but thankfully Carson was not. Carson would be diagnosed by professionals as autistic, as doctors did away with the Aspergers diagnosis years later. Michael had it so rough, and I did not help in any way. Life for him was hell. He did not have that many friends, partly due to his lack of social skills. Because he was challenged, certain family members bullied him with physical, sexual and verbal abuse, and he also endured excessive bullying in school. Because he was a special needs child, I can now see that he was beaten into normal, facing discipline with the rod for things he sometimes knew were wrong, but mostly more for the things he didn't know were wrong. In fact, when you look at someone who is autistic or even someone who has Down syndrome or even Tourette Syndrome, you will find a lot of their actions are not planned. They are impulsive and involuntary.

Now, this is not to justify all the actions one would do as a child and as an adult. I'm saying that for those who don't understand what is entailed in an autistic life. Michael received so many beatings that I lost count of how many he endured. If only I had understood what Michael was going through then... he was just trying to survive. My mother was hard on him for no reason. I don't know if she was trying to change him or thought she could do it on her own. All I know is that it caused depression for him, and it made him feel like he would never meet her expectations. Even if he did, it wouldn't have mattered. She would've wanted him to be whatever she wanted him to be.

This ties into this journal entry from Michael:

Michael's Journal
January 19, 1988:

Janice came up to me in full-blown conversation mode: "My man has never gone through anything that you've been through. You've been neglected, and that's probably why you get angry at sporadic moments, right?" I said yes. I don't plan it, and I don't like it when it happens, because I become very depressed and apologetic. This is partly why I'm in counseling.

But I questioned her too, "Is this your main reason for dropping me, because I'm not stable? Does my counseling and my cries for help matter?" Janice didn't waste any time making it plain. She said even if her parents were OK with interracial dating or marriage, I have too many issues. She claimed to know a lot of people who have problems and that she loves them "equally," but she's still trying to "wrap her mind" around the fact that she loves me - the JACKED-UP friend with a mental disorder.

Present Day:

I need to stop for a moment... this is making me cry!

Okay, I'm back. I just needed a breather. One thing I can say about Carson is that he shares many of the same traits as my brother did. Maybe this is what haunts me from time to time, seeing my deceased brother in my son:

1. Music, songs and when each was released. They are very good with dates and can more than likely tell you what was going on in their lives when they hear certain songs; such as the year when they came out, what grade they were in, and who wrote or produced the song.

2. Books read: If you are not careful, Carson might recite a children's book from beginning to end.

3. Movie clips and/or TV shows: Carson can quote lines verbatim. It is like a fixation.

Some of these are characteristics of autistic persons. And while I know that now, it still reminds me so much of my brother. Michael's life was nothing short of a punching bag. He was hit in the face quite often growing up, regardless of if it was his parents or Uncle Woody, the same despicable man who abused him and my Carson.

Near the end of his life, Michael had written that he could do five things right, but the one thing he would do wrong would be held against him for as long as he lived. This replayed in his mind, as our parents would glorify those wrongs. Though he had been in trouble too many times, he was the type of person who sought to make amends. But most of the time that was a dead end. I know most of the people who knew Michael knew that he apologized way too much. I see the same thing in Carson. It is the conscience within him that tells him that he is always doing something wrong, unintentionally hurting people who he so deeply loves and respects. It is only natural for him to feel that way, because his wrongs were magnified so much when he was younger. It hurt him immensely when he did not know that he had hurt someone, and they just stop talking to him. Having been rejected because of his neurodivergent state and abuse, he was thankful to have found stability in my faith. But at the same time, no man is on Gilligan's Island alone.

Let me get back to Carson's journal.

October 12, 2006:

My mom told me that I have autism. She told me that my uncle Michael may have had it too. That means I will be going to therapy once or twice a month. And my mom apologized for how she treated me for many years. She hugged me and asked me to forgive her.

I asked her what autism meant. She said that I think differently than most people; some people will appreciate it, and some will hate me.

"There are certain things you will need help with, and there are certain areas where you are special and may need assistance. I will be with you every step of the way from now on," she said.

Present Day:

Now, my heart cries for the state of our country and how we treat autistic people. We neurotypicals tend to expect autistic people to be like them, and that's not fair to them. We don't appreciate each other's uniqueness. They can contribute in a significant way, and Michael had a lot *of promise within him. It was stolen from him by his own parents. I vow to not let that happen to my son!*

December 12, 2006:

As my mom and I are getting ready for Christmas, we decided to decorate the Christmas tree together and listen to Christmas songs. It's something about them that makes me feel great!!!

GENOBIA

December 18, 2006:

I befriended Genobia and she was telling me a few things about her life. I was so concerned for her that I went to my mom to talk to her about this.

January 7, 2007:

Mom wanted me to ask Genobia if she wanted to have dinner with us so that she could meet her. Genobia said yes, and she came over. Brother Freeman came over as well and we all had my favorite dish, lasagna, along with mom's famous cheesecake.

My mom started the conversation once dinner was over. She asked Genobia, "what's going on? My son seems very concerned about you."

Initially, Genobia tried to fight it, until Brother Freeman told her this is a safe space.

"I know about Carson's abuse, and he's dealing with the trauma," he said. "I understand you both met at a support group and I know the facilitator." Genobia started to speak, yet she was shaking a little bit. My mom held on to her hand so that she could freely speak.

Genobia began to share her story with us. She said:

"When I was in kindergarten, up to that point, I thought my grandfather was my father up until this point. I struggle with school. It's not difficult; there are days I do good, and there are days when I zone out. There are times, I think there are about five people living inside of me, and it scares me at times to the point that to escape, I would have to die to get rid of each person. I heard about Jesus, yet I have my struggles with those people that may be living inside of me. Losing my grandmother was tough, she was the only person in my family that cared for me. In fact, she was praying for someone to save me, her granddaughter. Maybe she knew that my life was not going to be easy if I were to keep living. I'll be honest, this fight is no different than my love for Jesus – especially if I have to work my way into the third heaven, known as the celestial kingdom."

When Genobia left, Brother Freeman and my mom had a conversation. I had to get ready to go to bed; however, I overheard the conversation they had. They are concerned about Genobia and her potentially being schizophrenic; yet, this was not by her doing. Brother Freeman said those people living inside of her must be the people who harmed her body and they say that these are soul ties that have damaged her soul. He said this is one of the main reasons why this sanctuary is needed in our church. He told my mom to befriend her and be the mother she needs, if she allows it. He said Genobia needs somebody whom she can confide in and feel safe.

"In this world, there will be no safety for her, and I hate to say that she won't survive. I'm not trying to speak death over Genobia; I'm just stating the truth," he said.

June 20, 2008:

I thought about what Brother Freeman was trying to do, create a sanctuary for those who are suffering from mental health issues, and how to apply faith to those deep holes in their hearts. I remember two girls, Erica Coleman and Cheri Brown, in our support group who shared with us that they were either sexually assaulted or sold to different guys at the age of five years old. I remember when they shared, I cried for them, and when it was over, we gave them hugs and exchanged numbers to keep in touch with them. I believe Brother Freeman needs to talk to them; so, they can be a part of this sanctuary alongside me and many others who need it. I'll try to get in touch with him about them so they can be a part of it as well.

July 15, 2008:

My mom bought me Adele's 19 CD, and I like every song on it. I have to say that my personal favorite is "Right as Rain." It just has that nice live appeal to it.

Present Day:

I thought Adele's "Right As Rain" should have been a hit. I must agree with Carson, it is one of her best songs. I have learned that many songs that aren't radio singles are usually the better song.

October 5, 2008:

For the next counseling session, we talked about self-harm. We were asked if we have ever done that, and what are ways to not do that. Genobia and Melissa stated they had done it. They stated they were cutters, mainly their thighs, where it wasn't seen by others. During this session, Genobia mentioned that she was fascinated with monarch butterflies. The facilitator said, for the benefit of those who didn't know, that the butterfly is a symbol of transformation, change and endurance, because of its metamorphosis from a caterpillar to a butterfly.

October 5, 2008 (later that evening):

Later, I called Brother Freeman to tell him about the monarch butterflies, and he said that for many cultures and some religions, they could be considered as angels from the spirit world that carry the souls of their deceased loved ones. He said, in his opinion, they have spiritual meanings for some; however, it could be occultic if we put our trust in them. I asked him his thoughts as to why people cut themselves. He said those people are labeled as "cutters," and many do it to numb the pain they're feeling because of the trauma they've experienced. Sadly, it can be very addictive yet dangerous at the same time. It makes him cry that they're inflicting more harm to themselves. I said that it makes me cry, too.

FAMILY REUNION

February 20, 2010:

My mom came home with Sade's new CD Soldier of Love. She would not stop playing the title song as well as "Babyfather!" Even though she played those two songs constantly, I liked them.

July 4, 2010:

It's family reunion day. My mom told me to get ready, as we are traveling to New Jersey for this reunion. I asked my mom if Uncle Woody was coming. She said he's in jail for drug trafficking; so, he won't be there. I was so relieved. Sadly, Nanna is doing all she can to get him out of jail, but Papa is against it, and thankfully he wins against Nanna. I was able to meet siblings that I never met before, and it was such a great feeling to meet them. Now, I can learn more about my family tree.

SENIOR YEAR

October 12, 2010:

I read some of Michael's poems from his journal and was inspired to write something, as Jennifer is on my mind. I don't know if I'll give it to her, but we'll see. I call this "If You Could:"

If you could touch my emotions,
then you would understand how I feel,
If you could see the tears I cry,
then you would know my love is real.
If you could know the thoughts I think,
then you would understand
how much you stay on my mind,
If you could touch my hand,
then you would see a love that we could find.
If you could talk to me,
then you would understand the words I say

If you could spend time with me,
then you would know
I would want to be with you each day.
I see that your heart is tied to someone else
And I know that I seem selfish
when I say I want you for myself.
Understand that if you could do better,
I could do better, too,
But I don't want better,
because I'm only better with you.

May 6, 2011:

Despite the objection of my Nanna and Jennifer's father, Jennifer and I went to the prom together. I'm grateful that my mom is okay with us going to the prom together. I had a great time, and we just enjoyed the music and dancing and our time together. Songs like "Party Rock Anthem," "Rolling In The Deep" and "Till the World Ends" kept us on the dance floor.

May 8, 2011:

I think I have decided what I want to major in when I go to college. I want to double major in accounting and real estate at Georgetown University. I remember Jennifer telling me that she wanted to major in Early Childhood Education at Brigham Young University. So, that means we're going to be apart. I'm going to miss all the times we would just watch TV, the times we would just cuddle during movie time.

Present Day:

I was so proud that Carson went to Georgetown, and he is a successful accountant and has multiple real estate companies as clients. Because he knows the numbers, he tells the truth and will tell people if the investment is worth it or not.

I swore that I would not treat Carson the way my mom treated Michael. I became Carson's cheerleader when it came to his dreams and goals and I made sure that he got educational support so that his dreams could be realized. He should go further than I did, and that's what my father wanted for Michael, despite my mom competing against Michael and me.

June 1, 2011

I'm getting ready to graduate from high school. Wow! How the time flies. I'm so happy, but I'm also sad because Jennifer is leaving the state. She got a scholarship at BYU, and I'm going to Georgetown University. When we got our cap and gowns, much to my surprise, Jennifer came over to kiss me. I didn't know whether to scoop her up in my arms or to ask her if I could kiss her back. I did the latter, and we shared a passionate kiss. I have never been kissed like that before. I feel so loved, I decided to play some eclectic Jazz on YouTube, and the first song that came on is "Dawn" by Nite Flyte. Very soothing and relaxing, to where I feel like I'm floating on a cloud. I guess that sums up how I feel at this moment.

DEATH

August 1, 2011:

This was one of the hardest days of my life, and I'm sitting here thinking about my future, and two things. The first thing is I found out that Genobia took her life, and the second thing is that Jennifer, who I loved so dearly, cut off communication with me! If I could just roll up in a ball and die, I would.

I went back through Michael's journal, and as I was feeling what he was feeling when he went through his heart break, I started crying. I could not believe that what I was going through, he experienced it also. Wow, there are so many people who are going through what we go through, yet we will never know. I am supposed to be preparing for college, now that I'm finished high school, yet it seems to be a year of depression. I hope my adult life is better than my childhood. Thankfully, my mother believed me when she got the truth about Uncle Woody. It is sad that my grandmother and I do not talk. People in school looked at me like the village idiot and like I did not belong. I know I am so different, but does it give people the right to treat me like this? Maybe, I will know the answer later in my life. I guess, now, I must keep living, though it is hard. I wish I could find some form of happiness in my life at this moment.

As I sit here and think about it, I'm still trying to figure out what I could've done. Although my mom said to me that I did the best that I could for her, she was broken from the inside out. I can imagine Brother Freeman saying there was too much darkness that was permeating her life and preventing her from experiencing the love and healing of Jesus. Between the time I befriended her to this day, there were moments that she would go no contact with me.

I remember we used to talk about her writing in her journal, and she even said to me that she considered writing a screenplay, if not a book, about her life experiences. She wanted to let the world know what the reality of this abuse could do to a child. She was terrorized to the point that her mind and spirit were broken. Sadly, the devil took over her spirit because of the terror she experienced. My prayers could have only done so much.

Present Day:

I can say that suicide is the saddest thing to ever happen to a person, in my opinion. I think about Michael and now Genobia. Suicide was a permanent escape from their temporary pain. For some, that pain is torture for a person's being, whether it be physical, mental, spiritual or emotional - so the way out for them happens to be that.

I'm not saying that's the right thing to do, I will say that it's not the answer. Suicide does leave scars for some people, and then there are some who just carry on with their lives. When I think about that, it's sad that many would carry on, yet would want empathy and/or sympathy when something happens within their family. Talk about selfishness at its finest.

I remember when Genobia and I were talking; she was telling me about monarch butterflies and her love for them. I had to research what that was, and I found out that the term monarch is really about mind control. Wow. Most abusers have mind control in mind, and that can wreak massive havoc on their victims. Sadly, abuse is generational, and I agree that curse can be broken. I look at my family tree. Uncle Woody molested my brother and my son. The question now becomes; was Uncle Woody molested or perhaps my mother was molested? Especially for her attitude to be so full of hatred especially toward men. I'll never know; nor should I let that stop me from breaking that cycle. Michael was committed to breaking the curse, and I know Carson is determined to break it.

My father made Carson a CD of his favorite singing group, The Temptations. Carson played two songs constantly after hearing the news about the breakup with Jennifer: "I Wish It Would Rain" and "I Could Never Love Another." I would check on Carson to see if he was okay. He would say he was, but I knew he wasn't. It's a mom's nature to care for her child.

Although everyone grieves differently, it's still grief. It must happen, and I told him that if he needs me, I'm here for him. It's so important to say that, for them to know that someone is there if they need them.

It's funny; when I look back at when Michael got his heart broken. The way my son is feeling mirrors Michael, minus the fact that Michael played Sybil's song "Make It Easy on Me," constantly. Even though I was tired of the song, my father and I loved the song just as much.

I remember praying for Carson, because Brother Freeman told me that when music is turned on, it's usually a cry for help. There were so many songs that Carson was listening to, and these were songs that my father had listened to on a regular basis.

Okay, let me get back to sharing Carson's Journal.

August 10, 2011:

I wanted to hear some smooth jazz, so I put on some Peter White, and the first song that came on was "Romance Dance." Oh, I forgot to tell you what Jennifer said in her e-mail to me from August 1, 2011:

"Carson, let me just cut to the chase. I think you're immature and that the way you act around my friends is appalling, to say the least. You should have been in remedial classes for the way you act. And the things you say are so off-putting that even I feel disgusted to be around you. You should know by how I'm writing this, and this will sound cold: you are not my type. I need a man who can give me the things I want *when I want! And you're just not it! You are an embarrassment to my friends, and that is unacceptable. I would never want to be with a guy like you. This is the end!*

P.S. - Your religion isn't mine. I can't believe what you believe—and besides, our book of scripture is true and complete, unlike the Bible. I believe the Bible to be the word of God as far as it is translated correctly; and ONLY that far."

The song that immediately came to mine was sung by a 70s group called The Independents, and the song was called "Leaving Me." I guess you could call me an old soul, but that song summarized the total shock that I was in. I believe what caused this disagreement was the fact that I said that I loved her, and she was meaning to say that we both had to feel the same way. Based on how she had previously treated me, she gave me the impression that she loved me, especially with how much time we had spent together. I felt that she was my first true romance. I don't understand the mixed signals that she gave me. I will admit that it can be a struggle for me at times. I'm at a point in my life where if people can't love me, then they should just leave me alone. Sounds like a song my Papa loved by the Friends of Distinction. I believe it's called "Love or Let Me Be Lonely." I listened to that song after hearing "Leaving Me" and it just soothed my troubled mind.

August 11, 2011:

The more I think about it, I remember Jennifer made a comment to me about how her father made it clear that, in the Bible, it's written in Genesis 7 that Black people were a part of the seed of Cain, as Blackness came upon them. I didn't believe that, and maybe that explains why Jennifer called me a bigot. Because I didn't believe it, I was an outright bigot in her eyes. To me, that was hypocritical, especially since her father has the mindset that I am cursed. It's like he is saying that I should be dead on the spot. But it does leave some questions for me as to how Jennifer really felt about me, and what was the real motive behind her actions toward me.

August 14, 2011:

We had a support group meeting, and we talked about death. We first had a moment of silence for Genobia, and then we started talking. Erica started first and she stated that she was staring at death when her father put a gun to her face as he would rape her. Cheri expressed to us that her ex-boyfriend John Stallworth shot himself after the reality of their breakup sunk in. John's sister called Cheri and said that he shot himself in their garage. The bullet was inches away from his heart.

I cried immediately as the words were coming out of Cheri's mouth. It was like, I was living in the moment of being shot and blood everywhere. Between Genobia, Jennifer, and hearing Cheri's story, it did something to me. And then hearing David Ruffin's song in my head talking about placing a gun to his head was weighing heavy on my mind and spirit. Sure, placing a gun to my head seems like the easy thing to do, but I know I can't do that, even though the song "My Whole World Ended" is screaming in my head.

The facilitator said that explains why John isn't here as well. He has been missing a few times. He asked us to stop for a minute and write your feelings down on a piece of paper and then we'll read them before we dismiss.

August 14, 2011 (later that evening):

Brother Freeman had me listen to a song from William McDowell entitled "Give Us Your Heart." The only time I heard of him was when my mom would play "I Give Myself Away." In that song, he mentioned that they just made a declaration; so, I was trying to figure out what song was the declaration. I finally pieced that puzzle together when I heard the intro to "Give Us Your Heart." The intro was very enlightening and I agreed that I've been chosen for such a time as this. As the actual song played, I was in tears throughout the entire song. This song describes my heart and how I desire to live for the remainder of my days here on earth.

Present Day:

I understand why he was crying. It was like God was speaking to him through William McDowell. For the assignment on his life, he's built for this and truly made for this especially in such a time as this. Sadly, so many people run from the hard things looking for the easy way out. As for Carson, no walls will confide him. He is destined to make impact and change the world.

STEPHANIE'S MARRIAGE

August 25, 2011:

After asking me if I was interested in going to Hawaii, my mom threw me a curveball and told me that she's getting married. Because of where she works, she was able to get a hotel at a great rate just off Waikiki Beach. After seeing the website, I told her that I'm in. But I have my reservations about this man she's marrying. Knowing that my mom is all about her independence, she may lose that with him. I can see that in my spirit.

December 8, 2011:

We're in Hawaii, and it was a long flight. The hotel is awesome and the beach gives me the feeling of paradise. All I can hear in my mind is Sade's "Cherish The Day." I think that song has the right vibe for the scenery here.

Oh, right before I left home, I saw on social media that

one of my best friends is getting married. Based on where I am, I'm not mentally stable to attend. I explained to him that I went through a breakup, and I'm having problems with life. I let him know that I got his back, and I pray for a successful marriage. I didn't want to spoil his happy day because of what I'm going through, emotionally.

I must give my mom credit. She didn't invite the entire family, and I'm glad for that. It's just her, her husband, and me. I'm glad Nanna didn't come, because she was going to ensure that Uncle Woody came. I really wonder, can Uncle Woody do anything for himself, or is he going to continue to leech off Nanna? What I failed to mention about my stepfather's family is that they are straight hood or unpolished as some might put it, and they will fight over anything.

December 10, 2011:

Today, my mom is getting married. I've got bittersweet feelings about it, as I don't trust him. It was like she went from one boyfriend to another, and then out of nowhere, this man is promising her the world. I know I need to respect my mother's decisions; yet, I refuse to silence my opinion. For now, I'll keep it to myself. I'll come back later and share more about the day, as I know I'm not in my right mind mentally.

Well, the day went just as I expected. Everyone was happy except me. I still can't believe, or maybe I can, that Nanna invited Uncle Woody nor that she bailed him out of jail. My mom kept her composure together and did everything possible to not let her feelings show. The truth is, not only do I not trust my mom's husband, I don't even like him. He has a tendency to slap her around. And now that I'm older, I have found myself going to the gym more to really defend myself and my mom. It's one thing to have to fight Uncle Woody, but it's even worse now to have to prepare to fight my mom's new love interest. This can't go on for me. I'm already dealing with a lot. Adulting is no fun, so far!

I will admit, I may be considered emotionally unstable at this time. I'm still heartbroken after losing Jennifer, and to be honest, I want somebody to love me for me and not just see me as an ATM. It's cool that I'm being that friend that people need from me, but apart from that, they don't see me as "marriage material." Yet, they will turn around and yoke up with a man who couldn't rap their way out of a paper bag, and then they're divorced within a few years. And yes, these are women who "love the Lord." My attempts for maintaining integrity with women meant nothing, especially when I would declare that I'm saving myself for marriage.

Present Day:

One thing I can say about Carson, he's very protective of me. He'll speak his mind, and then lets it go. The more I think about it, I've met so many men throughout my life that have either tried to take advantage of me, this includes single and married men, and there was one was who so sweet to me, and I just cut him off because he was too kind to me. The irony is that he didn't want anything from me except to be a good friend. Looking back, I realize that was God really showing His love for me, yet I was too caught up with the men who have sought only one thing after me. Why we have to go through the school of hard knocks will always be a mystery to me. Thankfully, I was one who found God in the midst of my foolishness.

There are many who will turn their backs on God, and even blame Him under the mindset of, "why didn't He protect me?" Well, we make choices, but we have no say so about the consequences. We're in a day where people are searching for peace and the world is going to give it in a way that's going to be detrimental for their eternal soul. The world can try to come up with their own definition of God, but He is not like man, and He loves each of us with a love that no human could ever do. The key is for us to trust. Now trust is hard especially if you've been hurt by man, which I know I have. At the same token, I have to take responsibility for my choices, which for many, that will be a daunting task, as blame-shifting is easy to do.

That's what I love about Carson. He is just like Michael and has a heart for people. What saddens me at times is that the people who are around them aren't able to appreciate the type of men that they are. They really desire to please God and that have no ill intentions towards them. The tragedy is not everyone is able to appreciate men like them. They are the type who will get blamed from the past mistakes that others have done to them. God is truly on their lives, as they understand that most of the problems they have are caused by them. When I say them, I'm referring to men. Carson is very vocal about men being the cause of the problems that women have. In fact, I laughed when Carson said that *some of these men need their backs broken for how they play with women's hearts and do not even provide for them or the children they create with them.*

The more I think about it, sometimes we ladies hurt the very one who loves us because of our rose-colored glasses. We have to stop thinking that we're going to be treated the same with every man we have an interest in. That mindset is limiting our capacity. Ladies, we need to proceed with caution, not out of fear, but with an awareness of power that you're protected and loved by a Father who will never hurt you.

Anyway, I've digressed. Let me get back to his journal.

January 1, 2012:

It's a new year, and I don't want to live anymore. I told my mom that I'm tired of living and I'm not sure of what I might do. Losing Jennifer and Genobia gave me a feeling that I can't live anymore. Some people say it's selfish, but what gives people a reason to be cruel and not consider the feelings of others? I can't cut myself, because I don't like looking at my own blood. I'm not a fan of lighters or matches and try to avoid them. So, I'm not sure what my other options are. Maybe people would be happy if I weren't here.

January 5, 2012:

I called Suicide Prevention and the call was strange. I felt very dejected after talking to them. I treat them no differently than people in church when you ask them for prayer. They both really didn't want to take the time to listen to me. My thought is this: if I had a gun to my head, and all that's said to me is that "I'm sorry," or "I'll just pray for you," that just goes to show that they don't give a flip about me. I feel so alone, and people have turned their backs on me, just because I was a victim of childhood abuse, and the list goes on. Sure, they can say it's all in my head. Yet when it's heard constantly, that's called gaslighting.

Present Day:

I can't remember if I called Janice either in January or February of that year, but I knew that I needed to talk to her to see how she was doing, and also to see if she could help Carson with what he was dealing with. When I called her, I asked her how she would describe Michael. Janice shared a lot with me, and she said there's a part of her that felt guilty for treating him the way she did.

TRAYVON

February 26, 2012

Wow, Trayvon Martin was shot. I don't understand what this world is coming to. Is anybody safe anymore? And to think, he was only 17 years old. With everything going on in my life, I would've rather taken the bullet. I feel so alone. One day we will all be free, yet I'm reminded of Brother Freeman, when he quoted Jesus by saying, "in this world, we will have tribulation." And that is definitely the truth.

SOLITUDE

March 3, 2012:

I cannot wait until spring break. I need to get away and find some time alone to deal with the loss of losing Jennifer, and how no one is here to listen to me. I guess if I cannot get to Ocean City now, I'll listen to some calming music like Diana Krall's version of "Walk on By." One of my favorites is Peter White's version of the same song. Those songs will allow me to go to Ocean City in my mind! Losing Jennifer was hard, because I thought we had something special, especially when we were around each other. I can relate to Michael's journal when he wrote about this in his March 30, 1990, entry:

Michael's Journal
March 30, 1990:

It is talent show night again. This time I sang Michael Bolton's "How Am I Supposed to Live Without You." Of course, I announced that this was dedicated to someone in the audience. I'm sure everyone in the audience knew it was for Janice. I barely survived the second verse, because tears were flowing down my cheeks. I got through it, and Janice gave me a hug.

Present Day:

Wow, when I think about Diana Krall's song "Walk on By," I know Michael would have loved that style of music. Bossa Nova has a Calypso feel to it, and it can blend with R+B music. Yet, it sounds so much better in contemporary jazz. Bossa Nova would have been calming for everything that he was going through. Do not get me wrong; his love for music was amazing. In fact, I had to create playlists based on what he wrote in his journal. There are times I need to go down memory lane, especially from the dances I attended and the routines my girlfriends and I would do. One year, I was Homecoming Queen. When I obtained that, I thought I was all that and a bag of chips.

The more I think about it, this was around the time Carson got his driver's license. Wow, I know Carson was so excited when he did. Thankfully, because he was an introvert, he only had a few friends. Let me continue with this journal entry.

March 3, 2012:

Michael's writing is really moving. He sure had a way with words, and his music taste is amazing. Although I did not know him, I find myself inheriting his gifts. Let me put on

Benoit/Freeman's "Via Nueve" and see what I can write, especially with all these bottled feelings I have inside.

It's too cold to go to the beach now,
But I'll get to Ocean City somehow.
In the meantime, I'm there in my mind,
Hoping that peace of mind
is what I will find.
Between my mom getting married
and my woman I love dumping me,
All that I see is the sand, and wow,
the ocean just flowing so free.
If only the ocean would just take me away,
Then I would be free,
as I have no reason to stay.
I hear the music of an orchestra
and an acoustic guitar,
Behind that, the acoustic piano is playing
as smoothly as the drive of a luxury car.
If I were in Florida, I would drive the A1A
It's nothing but beaches, and the scenery,
it would surely take my breath away.
Since all of this is in my head,
I will continue thinking about this scene
They say dreams become reality,
but now,
I must really get this room cleaned.
Sadly, reality has set in,
and my life must go on;
So, for tonight, I will say to my journal,
for now, so long!

GOODBYE

April 16, 2012:

I went to a therapy session, and my therapist told me that I need to write an imaginary letter to Jennifer as a way of letting her go. I questioned why, when she's not going to see it. Jennifer just stopped talking to me without a care, if I lived or die. Is that how people are today? They just don't care if you live or decide to take your own life?

My therapist said:

"I'm sad to say this, but many don't care and won't care if people take their lives. This is just the selfishness of people today. Back to the task at hand, I need for you to write a letter to Jennifer and then just let her go. Set her free."

As it relates to the letter, I'll write it in my journal. I know this is going to help someone. So, here it goes:

"Dear Jennifer, the way our friendship ended hurt so much that I just wanted to hang myself (or as the song goes, 'crawl up into a ball and die'). It breaks my heart that we

couldn't have the talk that I wanted us to have. Because I care about you and your heart so much, I don't want you to believe the lie you've accepted. And it's not just a lie about you individually, but it's a lie about who Jesus is. This prophet you believe in is fallen and self-created. For your life to be the way it's supposed to be, you must get the right Jesus before you get the right you. I know you're in Utah, but what concerns me so much is that close to 80% of women are sexually abused by someone they know. Jennifer, you know what I had to go through with Uncle Woody; so, I know that you know that the subject of abuse is close to my heart. To add insult to injury, 33% of men are abused by someone they know. Unfortunately, for my race we have a higher rate of sexual assault and incest, so you may not understand fully what my culture is about. That's the first barrier we have and is a layover from the vestiges of enslavement. The man you believe as Savior is not. Only Jesus is our Savior, not a fallen man who became exalted. The truth is that your religion is not acceptable to people like me. I would be just a convert, not born into your religion, nor am I from where you are.

Some people would say that time heals all wounds. I don't believe that would be true in this case, because when the foundation is corrupt, it will remain corrupt. I care for everyone, and especially those of my race. It wouldn't surprise me that if I were to attend your church where you are, people would look down on me or think I am inferior because of my race.

Jennifer, you know how much I loved you, and it hurts me that you wouldn't understand what I believe. There's so much freedom in Jesus alone, that you would be freed from every burden you've been carrying. One of the things that bothered me is that in one of your foundational books, it mentions that

Cain was cursed and the devil needed a representative on earth, which would be my race. I know we've talked about this next point, and it's something that I wish we could've talked more about. You had said to me that Jesus died on the cross but didn't pay for sins on the cross. In my eyes, the cross paid it all! The worst thing I would want is for you to be offended with what Jesus did on the cross for mankind. That would put you in a dangerous situation. It's sad to know that you only cared about getting married on the timetable that you had, and that when we would talk about what we believed, you would turn a deaf ear. I wish you the best and it hurts my heart to say good-bye to you. I dreamed of a life with you, and it makes me cry as I'm about to close this letter to you. I enjoyed the times we shared together, as I will never forget how beautiful you are to me, as you have moved my heart in a special way. Just know that I still consider you a special friend to me and if you were to call me, I would pick up the phone in a heartbeat, because that's how much you mean to me. With all that was said, I guess this is good-bye and I will miss you more than words can say."

JANICE VISITS

May 3, 2012:

Janice came to stay with us, and my mom was telling her about my breakup with Jennifer. I was in my room listening to my media player to take my mind off what was going on with my world. Janice came into my room to talk to me about what happened. She listened to me talk about it, and she said some things that hurt, even though it was the truth. She said that Jennifer had moved on, and she could care less how I felt, let alone whether I lived or died.

"Give her credit, she wanted to let you know about the new man in her life. Some people dump others with no explanation, or they will cheat hoping you would take the hint. The bottom line is that she moved on," Janice said.

Janice continued:

"Granted, I was that way with Michael, and I could've been more sympathetic considering he felt that I was God's gift to the world, and he loved me with a love that I wasn't

ready for. I've heard people say that they need a good friend in their lives and usually they end up kicking that good friend out of their life. And that's what I did with Michael.

Back to you though. There's no telling if Jennifer cares about you or not. I know this is a hard pill for you that you will have to swallow, but you're knee deep in the grieving process. Many people don't acknowledge this, but the grief of losing someone you love via a relationship is just as hard as the death of a loved one. Also, know that there will be people who will ridicule you, even in the church. If Michael were here, he would tell you that it feels like a death occurred, but unfortunately for him, he would take his life."

Stephanie interjected by saying that Michael had to endure those in the church ridiculing him that he felt that way, and they picked and chose who they wanted to care for. She said many of them didn't even care if Michael died or not; they were more focused on their respective seat in the church.

I said, don't I know it. Many in my small group ridiculed me and told me to just get over it. I mentioned that I thought about ending my life, and they didn't care to where they didn't even call or check on me. It's almost like they could've cared less if I lived or died. At the same time, if someone in their clique would have gone through what I was going through, they would have had a prayer meeting for them. So, I guess not being in the "in-crowd" is my fault.

Janice said it's not my fault, that I should look at the bright side. There are backstabbers in the "in-crowd" too.

"I can tell you this, based on what you shared with me about Jennifer, I was her in almost every way," Janice continued. "I lived my life in this bubble, oblivious to everything. And that's where her headspace is at. I find it quite interesting that she called you a bigot, when what she believes is full of *racism, courtesy of their founders. Where we are in this country is no better, and it's so sad. When I go to meet with him, I want you to come with me, so we can talk about what I'm doing now and fill you in about Michael."*

June 15, 2012:

I rode with Janice and my mom to go see Brother Freeman, and we talked about Michael and discussed what Janice is doing. A couple of things stuck out with me, and most of it was what Brother Freeman was saying. Many times, Janice was nodding in agreement.

Brother Freeman had this advice to give:

"Carson, the best thing you can do for Jennifer is to just pray for her. If God can save Janice, He can save anyone. This is not just for Jennifer, but for anyone you come across. Never underestimate the power of God. Unfortunately, when people join some faiths, many don't know everything there is to know."

Janice interjected and said, that some still won't tell you everything – just what they want you to know.

Brother Freeman continued:

"One of the red flags of any church that you go to is if they don't believe that Jesus' death on the cross was enough to get you into heaven. When He died for you, it was finished! Now we can walk in freedom. No need to carry any burdens – as our bodies aren't made to carry burdens, but for those to be casted upon Him."

He continued:

"You had mentioned to me that Jennifer said that she believes the Bible to be the Word of God, as far as it's translated correctly. The question I would pose to Jennifer, if she

were standing beside you, is what parts are translated correctly and what parts aren't? When you think about that phrase, what it's really saying is that the Bible is secondary to the Book of Mormon that Jennifer gave you. For many people, they live with that mentality. They will say that to fit the beliefs within their own mind, thus making the Bible subject to their thoughts. Not a good way to live!"

Janice said to me that if I were to marry Jennifer, I would face problems I could never have imagined.

"Think about this, you would not be accepted for the mere fact that you're African American," Janice said. "If they accept you, they're trying to erase the past. I was doing some research, and I have found that in some churches, they participate in ritual abuse. Case in point; there are girls who are abused by relatives within that religion. When I think about it, Michael gave me a challenge in his final letter to me. At first, I blew it off, but before the funeral, I decided to look at the books he wanted me to look at. And God did a work in me during my reading, and now I can see clearly that Michael had my heart on his mind, a great depiction of how God has my heart on His mind. My regret is that Michael isn't here to see the change in me. I would just give him the biggest hug that I could."

"I echo Brother Freeman in that all you can do is pray for Jennifer. Also, that she is loved by the true and ever-lasting God. To be frank, when I left that religion, I had to go to counseling because of how I felt. Most of those feelings were rejection and fear, primarily because of that particular church. Some have issued threats because of how I left, and of course they called me an apostate. I laugh now because I thought Michael was an apostate for not believing what I initially believed, but now I realize that he was right, and I'm

free because of the light Michael carried. He was showing Jesus to me, and now I understand. I said all of that to say that if Jennifer were to leave that religion, she would need to go to counseling depending on how long she'd been there."

Janice said to me that she received a revelation while she was at BYU. She wondered that if the original leaders were against people like you and Michael, then there's a strong possibility that this religion is racist in nature. She realized that the reason why she went to BYU was to please her father, and it's probably the same reason why Jennifer went as well.

Brother Freeman said to Janice that the reason why he gave her and Michael a Bible back when they both were in school is because he wanted them to have the truth that wasn't altered. And what many people don't know is that the book of Zephaniah was written by a Black man. What he was trying to say is that God has created every color and hue, and God can use anybody, regardless of skin color. What's so sad is that in their own religion and literature, they frown heavily on interracial marriages, and it's astonishing that they read this book more than the Bible, and it's actually recorded there. What concerned him in this day in age, is that so many people want to be prophets and they're telling half-truths, or their lives are so corrupt from the inside out. Sadly, many people will believe them to their deaths.

I couldn't believe it. Maybe Jennifer will have the epiphany that Janice had. And to think, their leader said that he did more to keep a church together than Christ did, coupled with the fact that the men can become a god and run their own world with their many wives; now if that isn't blasphemy, I don't know what is.

PAPA

September 10, 2012:

My papa passed away yesterday. They said it was lung cancer and renal failure. As I understand, he did hard drugs and smoked excessively. I will always remember him and how he encouraged me to treat a woman like a lady. My papa will always be my father. Let me stop here, and I'll write more tomorrow.

September 12, 2012:

I didn't write anything on September 11, 2012, as this is a sad day for this country. I wanted to just pray for the families who lost a loved one. So, here I am today, writing, and my grandma is raising a fuss about my papa's insurance. I'm sitting here thinking that my grandma should be grateful that he left her with $1M in insurance. But no, she's upset that he didn't leave her with $2M. She believes that with everything he put her through, she's entitled to that amount. Never mind the fact that he was a husband, who loved her enough to leave her with something so that she would be better off. But from what I'm gathering, Nanna is probably not happy with her life. Considering, she now lost her husband, and her son died close to 20 years ago. According to my mom, she had nothing nice to say about her very own son. I will allow my mom some time to grieve as this is going to be hard on her. Before I go to bed, I'll just hug my mom and let her know that I'm here for her if she needs me.

Present Day:

I need to qualify what Carson is saying here. Although it's true my mother doesn't have a lot of nice things to say as it relates to certain people; now it bothers me how she degrades Michael in his absence. Having been able to experience his journal, I'm able to understand some of the questions that he had, especially why he thought a certain way, and why he felt the way he did at times - when he seemed so different. I don't think they diagnosed autism like they do now, but I would truly say that he was on the spectrum just like my son is. I'm glad we were able to detect that, and for Carson to journal, has helped in many ways. I believe that Uncle Woody and my mom put Michael through hell, therefore causing Michael to really be depressed many times. The pressure to have a girlfriend was weighing on him, and for Janice to break his heart, really pushed him over the edge. He really had a heart *for the people he loved, and he did everything he could to not overstep any boundaries with them. He knew how to love people unconditionally, especially when most of the people in his life took advantage of his kindness. Michael did not need harsh judgment. Michael needed treatment, understanding, professional help, and a supportive system.*

MELISSA

October 18, 2012:

At 6:00am, I logged onto my social media account, and I see the following on my newsfeed:

Melissa Stone: This is it! I can't live my life like this anymore. Don't try to call me, as I won't take any calls. I realize that I deserved my sexual assault and abuse, as I'm the one that caused it. If I mattered to my parents, and they saw me as special, this probably wouldn't have happened. I'm out of options, and I'm tired of fighting and defending myself from people who feel that I deserve my abuse. I'm a failure, and there's nothing that anyone can say to me at this point. This is my good-bye and my final post.

I reviewed the comments and was shocked to see how many comments that said:

"Rebuke that thought,"
"I am praying for you,"

"Stop saying that,"

One comment even said, "just go ahead and end your life!"

I was led to just go into her DM and say, if you happen to see this message, please call me. I left my number. Within a couple of hours, she called me. I said you have my undivided attention, talk to me; I'm listening.

"Out of all the people who left their number for me to call them, you're the only one I called," she said.

Melissa talks and I empathically listen:

"When you shared your story in the group, I had to share my story with you. I can't share my story with everybody, because not everybody can handle what I say. I've told a few people, and when I shared with the support group, I didn't tell the entire story. Over time, I resolved not to share it again because I have either been hated, or they told me to just get over it and forgive those who wronged me. Here's what happened to me, I was sexually assaulted by my father, and he's of the cloth. He passed me onto other church members as well. I was only 6 or 7, but I know that I was either in kindergarten or first grade. How this came to light was when I went to the doctor, they told me that I was tampered with down there. You would've thought it would have stopped, but my father continued to make it more painful because the doctor said what they said. They said I provoked all of this. So now I have razor cut all inside of my legs from numbing the pain I endured."

I sighed as I heard all of this. I'm not sure as to what to say about this. Within a few seconds, I ask, how can a child provoke an adult to have sex with them? That is extremely absurd and it's also a crime.

"I don't know, but there's a part of me that must protect

him and the church, or I will be blasted in church as a liar," she said. "So, I don't even go to that church anymore, and truthfully, I don't even know what to believe. Does God even love me and why did He allow this to me?"

I tell her, I know she has a couple of years left in college, and because she's so gifted, I ask her if she's thought about studying abroad. I was trying to see a way through her pain.

October 18, 2012 (later that evening):

I shared her post on my news feed primarily because I felt the same way she did last year. I told everyone that if they dared to call her selfish or stupid to keep their comments to themselves, as this is not the time or place right now. I had to do what I do on social media and challenge people's thoughts with some questions:

1. Why aren't people walking beside her?

2. Why aren't people praying for her

3. Why are people more focused on who is the next president?

Granted, I went through that, too, and I was told that I was too negative and that I should be thankful for the abuse.

Present Day:

Wow, Carson never told me about any of this. He just told me that he talked to Melissa and asked her if she thought about studying abroad. This was a lot to carry for both of them. He probably didn't want me to worry about her. He has such a beautiful heart for people who are hurting. He's that angel that so many people are touched by when they're around him. To be frank, I can imagine that's what happened with Michael, and he ended up ending his life because he felt the same way Melissa did. The more I think about it, what Melissa wrote is very similar to what Michael wrote in his suicide note. I had to check on Carson to see how he's feeling. He hugged me and let me know that he was able to calm her down. He told me that he shared with her that it wasn't her fault, regardless of what the perpetrators or anyone else said to her. They were trying to gaslight her and absolve themselves of any responsibility.

STALKED

October 19, 2012:

I was on a social media platform when I received a random inbox message from someone I once met at an event. I accepted her friend request, considering we shared similar pasts. Here's what it said:

Carson,

I just want you to know I am afraid of making a fool of myself in front of you...

but God talks to me and I feel that I have His approval, so I am confident in facing you right now without fail.

We were meant to be together, and I know this... you know this... and if you let me...

I am willing to spend the rest of my life with you. I want to be everything for you, to make you smile, restore love in your heart, kiss your pain away, cry your tears, be your sounding board, and sing to you (maybe not that).

It's true that I am in love with you. I have waited all my life to meet you, and you have finally come... Thank you, God! I tell you this: if you let me in your life, I will do everything I can to make you happy. With everything I have gone through, I can handle any storm. Even if you say no, I still won't turn my back on you.

I am always here. I am also willing to leave where I am at (like I said yesterday) with the clothes on my back... and my car! And I will move close to you, to my own place of course because I want to hold your hand... for the rest of your days.

If you let me... I can make you very... very happy and open a whole new world to you...

I am asking for a lifelong relationship with you; though, I'm not expecting you to fall in love with me. I may not be your type... and that's ok. I just want to be with you and I don't care how...

I need you and I never thought I would say that to anyone before, but I need you! It doesn't matter if I'm a friend... or more than that...

I am here to offer myself to you...

However, you may need me...

Please don't feel that I am desperate... I'm not!

I have everything I need in this world...

I live with a purpose... and my place in this world is very important...

I hold my own!

I can take care of myself well!

But I need you... and YES, you complete me!
And I would be the happiest person in the world...
if you stand beside me...
I don't ask anything else of you... but to stand beside me...
I will take care of the rest...
I mean this more than anything in the world...
I love you!
Please don't answer now...
Think about it for a little while...
and get back to me...
and if you run from me... I understand!
I will go on with my life...
Dani Michelle Thompson.

I was taken aback by this e-mail and was left speechless. This was a sweet e-mail yet scary. How could someone love me and they barely knew me? Let me just be a friend and as they say, proceed with extreme caution!

October 23, 2012:

I see two voicemails from Dani, each two minutes long, and I'm in total shock.

Voice message #1: "This is me, Dani. I just wanted to call and let you know that I apologize to you. So, I didn't want to just text, I wanted to talk to you and tell you that I'm sorry for the misunderstanding that I caused. It's kind of strange what I'm doing. I want to be around you. You know; I feel kind of strange because I've never done this before. So, I'm just coming to you, and I hope that I'm not making you feel uncomfortable in any way. If I am, please let me know. That's the last thing I want to do. If you get this message, just give me a call. It's hard for me, because I'm trying to move and start a new life away from my current boyfriend. I'm angry with him. I just want to hear your voice and know if you're okay. Just know that I'm always here for you. Again, I don't want to make you feel uncomfortable... that's the last thing I want to do. Again... I'm sorry."

I noticed at the very end it sounded like she was about to cry. I didn't know if I really wanted to hear the second voice mail. This was weighing down on me. I sighed as I played the second message.

Voice message #2: "Okay, so it's me again. I'm sorry. I just want to say that I know that I write a lot; so, I want to tell you, with my voice, that I'm telling you that I love you. I've waited a long time for you. I've tried to make sense of relationships that I have, the person that I am, and my place in this world. I don't know if I've ever had a relationship with anyone like you. I would be the luckiest person in the whole world, no matter what capacity the relationship may be. I just want to say that I love you and I take you as you are, whatever it may be. I just want to say I'm so sorry for crying. Call me back and let me know you're okay. I sound crazy, and I don't mind sounding crazy... it's worth it. So, call me. I love you. I care about you. I just want to be around you and just make sure you're happy; so, that you don't go through any more drama in your life ever again. I'm going to make sure of that. Okay, let me get off the phone now. Bye."

All that went through my mind after hearing her message was; you don't know me like that! You've waited a long time for me? Woman, you hardly know me. We met face to face one day, excluding the two weeks of talking via social media. What in the world is this?!!

November 5, 2012:

I told my mom about Dani and what has transpired as a result. I told her that when she sent me an initial friend request, she would unfriend me days later when I said something she wouldn't want to hear, mainly that we need to be only friends, since I barely know her. She sent another friend request and then unfriended me again. Then, for the third time, she sent me a friend request and then unfriended me. This time, I made the ultimate decision to block her.

I think my mom was ready to fight this woman when I told her that I woke up to a string of texts from Dani asking if I'm bipolar because I questioned her mental sanity. And these text messages were sent to me at 3 AM. Mom had me go to the police, and they told me to send a text to Dani saying if she texted me again, I would press charges against you. Once I sent it, the text messages stopped. I think I'll be able to sleep in peace tonight.

REVELATION

November 10, 2012:

I'm going to try to write a poem, and I'm going to entitle it BBB (Broken, Beaten & Battered):

I come to the Father broken, beaten & battered.
He wants all my pain.
I lay this broken body down as if it were dead,
So, it's Jesus I gain.
Loved ones have abandoned me,
but You, Lord, have loved me still.
I surrender my life to you in all areas,
and I surrender to Your will.
I spent so many years living for me,
and it has brought me nothing but sorrow.
So, I seek You and Your righteousness and will strive not to worry about tomorrow.
So many are living for self, striving for attention,

Lord, turn our hearts back to You.
We will keep hurting each other
if we keep doing what we do.
This life of abstinence is not for me,
but for Your glory.
Some will mock my testimony,
but You have given me this story.
The good that I do for others is nothing
but a filthy rag in your eyes.
So, why should I boast in it,
Your dying for me is where my faith lies.
If I must live this life alone,
broken, beaten, & battered;
I count it all joy; though, my life
feels like glass that's shattered.
All the pieces on the floor,
as no one cares to clean me up.
But You are the only one to pick me up
and overfill my cup.
I have loved and lost,
and I have hurt those I care about.
I pray they forgive me, and I thank You, Lord,
for not judging me and taking me out.
If you were brave enough to read this,
come to Jesus this minute, this hour.
He wants your broken, beaten & battered heart & spirit; so,
He can make your life beautiful as a flower.

Hey, that was pretty good.

April 10, 2013:

I received an inbox message on social media from Melissa; she received an invitation to study abroad in Germany. She will be studying medicine in Germany. I'm so happy for her, as she's very gifted in this area. I will miss her, but I know she can thrive wherever she is.

May 1, 2013:

I was talking to Brother Freeman as to why abuse victims aren't protected. Why are they put them back in a home where they are abused, and mentally destroyed? He said to me that we're in the world, and this world is all about destruction and destroying the next generation.

May 2, 2013:

I was thinking one day about this concept of abuse (especially for Genobia and Melissa), and why I'm so bothered by it all. Let's think about it for a minute in this scenario if I were a molester of children:

I have a daughter and molest her. The mother denies it and the abuse continues. The daughter gets married and pregnant, and her daughter is abused by her husband; so, she divorces him. My daughter has nowhere to run and comes back home to me, now exposing her children to a molester. My daughter is now bashing every abused victim, telling them they need to grow up and forgive people like me, and they need to get over everything that happened to them. Meanwhile, she is exposing her children to me, knowing what I'm capable of doing. People love and idolize my daughter and how she wants abused victims to forgive me. I don't have to say I'm sorry. They're supposed to apologize to me, since (in my mind) I still don't understand how what I did to my daughter was wrong. Let's be real, why would anybody even consider bringing their children around people like me, considering all the hell I put my daughter through. What would she expect you to forgive me for what I did? Boundaries should be set!

Present Day:

Wow, I felt so convicted after reading that. Carson is just as brilliant at writing as Michael was. Speaking of which, Michael loved talking to Brother Freeman, when it came to the church. Brother Freeman said this, and Michael was so into what he was saying as it relates to the church. He said that so many in the church are so focused on the 99 found sheep that they won't even pray for those who are lost. Jesus came to seek and save the lost. If we feel that reaching the lost is too hard, then we're not called. God has anointed us with His power; we just need to get off our complacent behinds and fulfill the great commission. Get up from your pew and lay hands on those who need a touch from the Lord. Most of them want to know the Lord, but they can't see because of the scales over their eyes. So, we need to stop cursing those who don't know the Lord, and we need to be the salt over the earth.

Many of those we're cursing have deep seated wounds - ranging from sexual abuse, domestic abuse, *ritual abuse. They need love. They don't need the hate based on the words that we speak to them.*

We say that we believe God, but if God put it in our spirit or dreams to pray for someone, we should be proactive. Pray for them, fast for them and intercede for them. Can we put "self" down and be obedient to what He wants us to do? That person needs to be free, just like you.

February 12, 2014:

I was talking to Brother Freeman today, as I was concerned about celebrities today. Many of them think they are role models and can speak to things that I've been through. What makes them more important than little people like me? He said something to me that was very profound:

"Carson, you must understand that abuse survivors in the church look to celebrities as role models, when in fact, many celebrities and/or counselors who have survived abuse give the impression that they have a chip on their shoulders. There's no sympathy to those who have suffered. Some have gone as far as attacking victims by saying 'you're in sin because you're not thinking right,' – regardless of what state they are in."

"That's not fair to an abuse survivor. Instead of attacking, even if it's unintentional, people with influence need to understand where people are in their path to recovery, and that they are still struggling with the pain of abuse. There's a well-known pastor who stated that she was abused by her biological father. He began with grooming behavior, then used manipulation, threats, coercion, and other fear tactics which eventually turned into molestation. The concern that comes up

is that when you're talking to a lot of people, such as in a stadium, the speaker must be mindful of who may be in the audience, and don't let the camera be on that person when they are triggered. That will not be a pretty picture."

"Whoever is teaching on a platform, there must be an option for people to feel safe, as church is supposed to be 'safe haven.' Hence, that's the reason for the sanctuary that is near completion! The pulpit is not designed for dumping your personal laundry on others. That needs to be done in a different venue. Testimonies are great, but when it comes to abuse, that needs to be handled with care. And the worst thing that a pastor can say when someone has been abused, is to 'get over it!' That's the fastest way to cause a trigger that can lead to running away from God or even worse, suicide!"

I'll be honest, many churches have been a disservice to abuse victims. Sad to say this, but Michael wasn't appreciated by his church family; however, they catered to their favorites. I said to Brother Freeman that in one of my small groups, a few people were going through what I was. They catered to them, yet I was treated like a second-class citizen. Brother Freeman nodded and say, not too much has changed. There are people in churches that will cater to their cliques while people are suffering in silence, and make you appear to be toxic. So, I completely understand when Michael speaks of the American Middle-Class church, where the mindset is about "me, my family, and my clique." Just like society, churches treat people who are different strangely, to the point of ostracizing them, despite the fact they are very gifted in areas where they are not. I said to Brother Freeman, it sounds like Michael tried to cast his cares on others, yet was unheard. Granted, there are times I'm not heard either.

What grieves me at times is that some people won't even sit down to talk to me, perhaps they would actually open their eyes and see me differently. Maybe that's what happened to Michael.

Brother Freeman said some of the people talked to him, but the ostracizing of the others was stronger than the positivity he received. And we have the audacity to tell abuse victims to not take offense, yet we are the ones doing the offending. This is why I pray that this sanctuary blesses those who have suffered like you and Michael and people who come will know that God loves them despite how people inside and outside the church act. I also pray that the people who come may not have a place in the local church, but they will know they have a work to do for His glory.

That was so comforting to hear. Well, let me close my journal for tonight.

March 23, 2014:

My mom filed for a divorce from the man she was married to. I'm glad she did finally. He just wanted to get as much money from my mom, and all he would do was drink, dictate and dabble in physical abuse with her. She could do bad by herself. The day she filed it, she pulled out her Mary J. Blige "Live from the House of Blues" DVD. I sat and watched it with her and especially enjoyed her performance of my favorite song, "Your Child." When Mary broke down, screaming and crying, I started crying, too, because I could tell that she was hurt. My mom wanted to make sure I was okay; so, I said I was fine. I thought back to my conversation with Brother Freeman about people bleeding onto others, and how no one is healed. Instead, they're re-traumatized.

Present Day:

My son is very protective of me. And I stated back then: he's going to be a great husband, as he's very protective of the people he loves.

September 20, 2014:

I asked Brother Freeman, why am I struggling, trying to find a woman that will love me? Has my abuse and my autism scarred me for life? Why are the nice guys finishing last? It's like women want to just be with these trifling men and then, after they've had enough of being misused and abused, they come to me. Some of them are so bitter that they blame me for the things that others did that I didn't do. Are we nice guys to take this punishment? Help a brother understand. And while I'm on that, where are the good men at to stand with me!? We need a resurrection of good men to come up!

He smiled and said this to me:

"I could write a book on what you just said. It's hard to find, because men like that are in the minority. God is still asking, 'Adam, where are you?' Men are missing in action due to the deception of the enemy. Think about it; if there is no man, where does the family go? You are not asking too much. I don't believe I asked too much when it came to finding a mate either. I told my wife I've run across too many women that couldn't rise to the occasion. I look for quality in a woman, someone who can hold her own financially, spiritually

and emotionally. It is the man's place to lead, but not in a domineering manner. The culture in the world today can't even define a man or a woman now. They have feminized our men. And in some cases, the woman wants to be the head. And that's sometimes due to having an absent father. However, there are some men after God's heart. Seek the Holy Spirit."

LISA

October 10, 2015:

I met Lisa Holmes at work today, and I think she is so fine. I am determined to not ask her out until I leave this job; that way I'm not in violation of the unwritten policy of workplace romance.

January 12, 2016:

I am leaving my job for another, and Lisa and I now talk, occasionally. She finds me very interesting, and we have a love for reading. So, I gave Lisa my number in the hope that she would call me and that we would read a book together. I also found out that she went to Georgetown University like I did. I told her that I double majored in accounting and real estate, and she majored in social work. When I said that, a moment of sadness came over me. Uncle Michael never got a chance to go to college, and I can imagine that was his one of his many dreams!

February 13, 2016:

I was just about to give up hope, yet Lisa called me and asked me if I had plans. I said I didn't, and I asked her out. She, thankfully, said yes. I had prayed that if she called, that would mean I had found my mate.

February 14, 2016:

Lisa and I went out to eat, and she shared her heart with me as I shared my heart with her. She told me that her mother kicked her out of the house when she was 16, and she ended up with a baby at 17. She gave her baby up for an adoption, and she knows the foster parents; so, she's able to see her baby when she can.

As the evening ended, I gave her a heartfelt hug and I kissed her forehead. I also let her know that she's lovable and I believe in her.

I resolved within myself to fight for her and to love her the way she's supposed to be loved. I'm not talking sexually, but I'm talking spiritually and emotionally. I know her heart and soul are wounded, but are in no way beyond repair!

Present Day:

Reading this entry really made me smile. Lisa is truly the best thing that has come into his life, especially with all that he's been through. He deserves that happi-

ness. He's had some struggles in his life, some were from Jennifer. Sadly, most came from my mom and Uncle Woody. I do feel bad that he had to hide it from me, but I understand why he felt that way because my mom and I were very close. We were more like sisters than we were mother/daughter. I do regret that now; yet, I'm glad that Brother Freeman and Janice were able to help him through the funk that he was in.

February 20, 2016:

I shared with Lisa my essay on living with autism for this contest that I'm going to enter into. She took my essay and spiced it up for me. She truly has a way with words, and I thanked her for doing that.

March 20, 2016:

Lisa and I were talking on the phone, and she told me when I was sharing what I went through. She said she is so glad I didn't commit suicide, as it's not the answer. I thanked her for being such a great friend.

April 11, 2016:

I found out that my essay ranked third in the contest; however, the judges wanted me to read my essay at the Honestly Autism Day event this up-and-coming Saturday, to which I accepted.

April 16, 2016:

I enjoyed Honestly Autism Day, and I read my essay at the event. Much to my surprise, the essay received a standing ovation, and I proceeded immediately to the back of the room and just fell on the floor to curl up in a ball so I could cry. I wasn't sad, just overwhelmed by the response.

Here's a little piece of the essay:

As a child, I was often ignored and even ostracized by my peers due to my lack of social skills. I was bullied by certain family members and fell victim to physical, sexual and verbal abuse. My mother didn't know how to work with me; since, she never had to deal with a child who wasn't normal. They tried to make me normal with discipline. Unfortunately, it didn't work. Once my mother had the understanding of what I had, she was very supportive and embraced me as someone very special to her.

I hope that my words and my work encourage parents to seek help for their children as well as inspire those living on the spectrum to realize that even in their differences they are special and are needed to make the world a better place.

I told Lisa about it and she was ecstatic that I did a great job. She has so much faith and confidence in me that I'm so glad I have her as my best friend and, in my eyes, as the love of my life.

September 4, 2016:

I took Lisa out for her birthday, and I was able to

surprise her with a dessert. How I did that was when she went to the bathroom, I told the server that it was her birthday. To see Lisa surprised brought such joy to my heart. I desire to make her happy, yet I know that she must choose to be happy herself. I just want to be an assistance to her in any way God sees fit. I guess this is the start of a romance for me.

November 12, 2016:

I asked Lisa if she wanted to go to a ballet as I have a love for classical music. She was hesitant, but she came with me.

October 12, 2017:

I asked Lisa to marry me. Much to my surprise, she said yes. I waited to go back to my apartment before I cried my tears of joy. I didn't want her to see me cry. I guess that's the man I am. And besides, what would she think of me if I cried in front of her?

November 11, 2017:

I asked Lisa if she could come with me to Arlington National cemetery, as that is where my Papa is buried. I'm so glad she came. I need to make peace with him knowing that he's not here to see the woman I'm about to marry. I told her a story that he told me when I asked him about his trophies. He said that he got them around the time my Uncle Michael was born. He had a singing group and there were four guys. They were at a talent show in Delaware, and they won first place singing "I'll Be Around" by the Spinners. The second trophy was for third place. That time they had a woman singing with them, and they sang "Where Peaceful Waters Flow" by Gladys Knight and the Pips. Lisa smiled to hear that, and said she wished that she could've met my Papa! I know he would've liked her and approved of me being with her for life.

Present Day:

I found out while I was at my father's funeral that my father's singing group had an opportunity to record at a studio in Philadelphia with a well-known Philly producer. I smile, as Michael loved Philly Soul Music so much. Now, I see the reason why he loved it, because our father played it a lot in our house. The reason why my father's group didn't record in the studio was because all the members were in the military, and a couple of them were moving to their respective locations as requested by the military.

December 25, 2017:

I broke the news of my engagement to my mom, and she was ecstatic. Lisa and I decided to get married in December of next year. We told my mom that my grandma can come, provided she doesn't bring Uncle Woody. And there will be no surprises either, where my grandma says he's not coming, but still brings him. That's only if he is out on bail. Who knows if he's in jail or not.

May 15, 2018:

I'm so happy that we have less than seven months left towards our engagement. To be able to marry the woman that I love is a blessing. I know we are going to make an impact not only on the world, but even on our families. We are going to show them that better is possible if they're willing to change their mindset and put in the required work to make their dreams come true. Of course, we know the decision is theirs. But as Sade said in one of her songs, "Nothing Can Come Between Us!" Being able to live out the teaching of my Papa, to treat my woman like a lady, warms my heart. Just seeing Lisa smile when I serve her just makes me want to take my serving to the next level! To me, Lisa is not just a lady; she's the queen of my heart! I'm a little heartbroken that Papa can't walk Lisa down the aisle for our wedding, nor be able to dance with her for the father/daughter dance. We would've played Luther Vandross' "Dance With My Father," as Papa had every album of his!

FREEDOM

July 3, 2018:

I had a talk with Brother Freeman, and he wants me to be involved with this sanctuary that he's finally completed, to run it with him. He told me that the only people who can really stop evil are "the church." However, the devil has poisoned many churches. The church has tolerated child abuse, domestic abuse, death of children by means of suicide and mutilation of children whether it be self-harm via cutting and or burning themselves. He hated to say this, but many in church are broken and internally bleeding; so, they're ineffective in helping others. He told me that I have enough experience with abuse and, having walked through that path, my testimony will speak so much louder!

I would also say to Brother Freeman that this may be my purpose in this life. I understand that we place blame on the victim, when it comes to abuse, because it's easy, and the perpetrators don't want to acknowledge their part. If they do, it's from a place of guilt. I've learned not to expect people to respond favorably when I'm neglecting how I say something. Everything spoken should be seasoned with salt. I just can't talk to people any kind of way, and granted, I don't want to be talked to any kind of way. To be honest, we must be proactive with our responses; then, people can respond correctly. This will clear up many of the miscommunications.

Brother Freeman agreed with me, and he said that we're in a place where culture has destroyed society and even the church. Now it's color versus color, denomination versus denomination, personality versus personality. It's no longer between evil or good, what's biblical or what is not. And if you disagree, then you're considered the enemy. It's a sad place for us to be. We are worshiping things, to the point of making them idols, and not Christ. We're more focused on what's going on in the culture and trying to change it on our own terms, without considering Biblical solutions. We are focused more on our personal agendas than we are on our Bibles, that we say we love. And this is why the world's problems aren't being solved, because people inside the church are fighting and destroying each other – with the simplest thing, our words! A well-known pastor even said that the church is the most racist organization, and it's so sad when it's to be a place of healing.

Before we left, I asked him if he would officiate my wedding, to which he said he would be honored!

November 9, 2018:

Before I turn over my journal to my mom, I want this to be one of my final entries for this journal. I don't know if I'll have any children or any sons to carry on my legacy. So, to be safe, let me impart this. There are so many things that are wrong with the family unit, and it stems from generational habits.

As a man, I want to stop this curse, here and now. This concept of "what goes on in the house, stays in the house," has its place; however, we have taken that concept and used it cover up abuse, thus traumatizing children, who will grow up to traumatize their kids. I saw it clearly in my family. My grand Uncle Woody would abuse Michael and Uncle Woody abused me. My Nanna abused Michael and there were moments in my childhood when my mom would abuse me. I would say that was due to what she saw being done in the house. This is the part that can't stay in the house. The problem in the end is not only repression, but also internal bleeding. It's similar to blunt trauma that can occur because of a car accident; though bleeding is not invisible, it's an internal loss, as it occurs from the vascular system into a body cavity or space. Many people don't realize this, but internal bleeding can happen physically, mentally, spiritually, and emotionally. I look at my life and Michael's life and realize that we were hit by a car and started bleeding internally on impact. Brother Freeman told me that what Michael and I went through was sexual abuse, and I know he prayed for Michael as he did for me. I appreciate Brother Freeman so much, and I'm committed to making an impact on my family for the better, so our legacy isn't totally tarnished. I desire to go on and acquire my certified public accountant license, and outside of my daily work, minister to those who are hurt because of familial abuse and even abuse from members of the church.

I pray for Melissa to understand that no child can consent to having sex when a child doesn't even understand *the concept of sex. I apologize to her and any other abuse victim who has ever encountered this.*

If my mom decides to share my journal to the world, and if you are one who has suffered child sexual abuse and been ostracized for speaking out against it, or perhaps, you have animosity towards God as a result of your abuse, I dedicate this portion of my journal to you.

Understand, if someone inside the church molested a child, it's not a godly act. It's demonic. The God I serve is a God of love and healing, never desiring to strip a child of their identity. I totally understand that your view of God may be warped because of the representatives who used God and abused their power to harm you, and to you, I apologize.

It grieves my heart when I even see people in church sitting in pews who are internally bleeding because they have been abused. Because the bleeding hasn't stopped, they're slowly dying, and we can't blame them when they isolate themselves and stop socializing with the church. If you have been hurt by the church, I apologize to you.

For a parent to neglect their child, reject or abandon their child, that will cause them internal bleeding. If the internal bleeding isn't addressed when it's first noticed, the ramifications could be costly. Church leaders who embrace wrong thinking and wrong living toward people who have unhealed wounds will cause people to die prematurely!

Is there's a compartment of your life that's especially painful and that you haven't opened to God? That's a question that I want you to think about. The beauty of God is that He will get our attention either by revelation or by a situation. Now, every situation is not your fault, though some might be, especially if it's sinful. But know this: His love for you has not changed, nor will it ever. If you were wronged like I was when

I was molested, it's not fair, and you are so right. Know that He does NOT cause evil, and I repeat: He does NOT cause evil. Evil exists and God can bring good out of it. The key is, now that you survived it, is to surrender to the process of healing. If you know Him, you will do it. He wants the broken pieces of your heart and spirit along with the negative thoughts you've been saying to yourself.

Also, know that there is a difference between where you are and where God wants you to be. I know that your pain has caused you to be depressed and has probably put you in a state of disconnecting to protect yourself. I understand that's where you are, but you must ask this: how will you change? You could go to a positive thinking seminar, have a mantra where you say/quote things, etc. The result is that you'll change some mental things and get some viruses out of your mind, know that it won't last nor be sufficient for what you really need. Keep in mind that I'm in the same boat as many of you who are reading this, but know that we're going to heal together. Now, this is going to sting, but you need to let God take over. But He can't take over until you let Him; you won't let Him until you love Him and you won't love Him, until you get religion out of your life and develop a relationship with Christ.

More than anything else, you must look deep into your heart and want freedom from the pain and any internal bleeding you suffered on an emotional level, mental level, physical level, and spiritual level more than anything else. How many of you desire that? I don't know about you, but I want freedom from it! One ticket to freedom is to disconnect from people who are a hindrance to your freedom, who want to sweep the carpet from under your feet and destroy your God-designed future.

Because you have been through something traumatic that caused you internal bleeding on the levels mentioned above, the enemy might have caused a lid to be put on you to say, "you won't go any further." If the enemy can cause you to focus on every mistake you made in your life, there's a strong chance that you will punish yourself. The God that we serve doesn't care about the mistakes you made. His love will never change.

November 10, 2018:

This day, I will turn my journal over to my mom. As I am preparing for my new life with my soon to be bride, I will not need this journal anymore as I consider my past gone. It's my prayer that my mom will be able to appreciate the beauty of life, and the son she raised and how I've grown. I'm grateful that she gave me this journal as it allowed me to get all my feelings out knowing that people who were supposed to love me were trying to kill me. And may this journal also be my testimony of God's grace over me amid the chaos I endured. With that, may she also see the love of God over me. Mom, I love you.

EPILOGUE

Present Day:

I still cannot believe that I have crossed the fifty-year-old threshold. As I think about what I've written, I now understand how Michael was feeling. He was trying to be happy, and he couldn't get to that place called happy. He thought having a girlfriend would make him happy, but they did not like him the way he loved them. Usually, they were trying to get what they could from him. One woman asked for money each week, and he gave it, only to get nothing in return, except to find out that the woman was pregnant. Of course, the money giving would eventually stop. I am glad that he found God before he passed away. The more I think about that, not only did he want to get to that place called happy, but he also really wanted to be loved by his parents, his friends and have Janice's love. I believe God loved Michael, and Michael loved God. The problem was that his pain was crying, if not screaming at him, and those screams took over. One thing I've learned in this life is that culture screams; God doesn't. In fact, God speaks in a still, small voice, and what's important is that we quiet our hearts so that we can hear it.

Now that I'm older, I try to remember the simple things in life, and I will always hold the memory of one beautiful, peaceful moment with Michael was in the summer of 1988, when we sat together and just listened to the radio. We both swayed to the melody of Dianne Reeves' "Better Days." followed by Billy Ocean's "The Colour of Love." Not only was the weather nice and hot, we were able to sit on the patio under the umbrella drinking iced tea. Uncle Woody was arrested for drug possession, so Michael was able to enter the eighth grade with peace of mind. No words were said, we just embraced moments like this.

It's funny that I remember before Michael passed, he dedicated a song to Janice on the radio. He swore on his life that he was going to marry her. How could I forget the song, it was Cathy Dennis' "Too Many Walls." To hear Michael's voice when he dedicated it made me smile. Initially, I thought he was a fool but, inside, I smiled because I liked the song as much as he did.

In hindsight, the biggest issue with Michael was that he felt unloved. The girls he liked didn't appreciate him, and his mother and father only saw the negatives that he did. He probably felt was he should not be offended when he was treated that way. He really didn't want to be the victim, though his mother frequently yelled at him from time to time that he was just playing the victim. The truth was he was victimized. Michael was diagnosed as autistic, and the world punished him.

My son is also autistic and is sometimes also punished by people who say they love the Lord. He's been through some difficult situations, but I'm so proud of him. As Michael said, Carson also is aware of the American Middle-Class Church concept. And now, to see my son married to the love of his life truly warms my heart. He's definitely a warrior and now, he's making his own path, knowing his gifts are outside the church walls. He knows he will never get the respect from people within the church because his personality is different. He wants excellence like his pastor, yet what is passed off as excellence in the church is mediocrity and it's accepted. He wants to fight the injustices, but he's not allowed to because he's not the pastor. My son has a pastor's heart and wants to fight the injustices, but he's not allowed to because he's not the pastor. The pastor is worshiped by some who are quick to judge my son and disown him because of his autism.

As I had to face my brother's death and for Carson who had to face Genobia's death, so many are leaving this earth unfulfilled. There are so many people in this world who are also stuck and judged unfairly, yet no one is helping them. My thought is this, why not leave with God and not take the risk of hell potentially being real? I know someone is wondering, why would a loving God allow people to die and why would God allow all the pain in this world? Well, I may not be able to answer it in a way that would cause the questions to go away, but I know that He is not the author of the confusion that is going on. God just wants people to love Him and trust Him that He knows all; you can choose to turn your life over to Him and not just your own understanding.

As for me, I would say my attitude does need some work. Granted, we all need to adjust our attitude, as agape (love) and honor are so missing in this world today. How do I know that I'm a piece of work? I still deal with anger, the spoiled brat syndrome, and pride. Growing up, I didn't like Michael, and I believe he was jealous of me. Now that he has been gone for 30 plus years, I still wonder how his life would've turned out. After reading his journal, and understanding some of the reasons he ended his life, my sensitivity towards people who even mention the word suicide has become heightened. I've seen people take their own lives because of childhood abuse, domestic abuse, and no one taking the time to listen to them. Why? Because we're so self-indulged in our lives. We focus on the "self" as being number one, and everyone else can go to hell. One thing I've learned is that if someone is crying out for help, and you're doing all the talking and not allowing the victim to get their feelings out, don't be alarmed if suicidal people get quiet and start to pull away. They won't say anything, even though they have given clues, and they will turn around and end their lives prematurely.

One thing is for sure: the process of healing is never easy. I think we need to stop being comfortable in our respective place. One of the problems I see, especially in the African American community, is this philosophy of "what goes on the house, stays in the house." My mom was a big proponent of it, and look at how divided our house became as a result. She swept a blanket over Michael's abuse and tried to do that to my son as well, doing all she could to defend Uncle Woody. This is the danger of deflecting, and it must stop. Somebody must break this chain of curses. So, this is one of the reasons my mom and I don't even talk. She refuses to take accountability or is afraid of admitting that she made mistakes. I will continually pray that her heart will open to the truth. The problem she has is no different than that of many people who are in leadership, the lack of accountability and not assuming responsibility for their actions nor the consequences.

Sadly, there will be some people who will get mad when people don't bail them out of the affliction that they themselves created. And they will assume no accountability for their actions, whatsoever.

My parents grew up in the hood and, thankfully, my father told me that he wanted out of the hood. He joined the military to get out of the hood. Thankfully, Michael and I didn't get to experience the hood that my parents went through, even though we visit it at times. But I remember a well-known motivational speaker said that the hood is very restrictive, and it can easily restrict your movement. I find that to be very true. So, if my dad made it out of the hood, so can anybody else. The hood mentality needs to change and people have to want better for themselves. Are there systems that create the hood? Yes. For every system, there is a counter to it, and we must find it. As I think about it, I cry because Michael never had children, and he was Gerald's last male child.

I still can't believe my mom said that my son is slow. If I were to confront her today, she would deny it. This is another cycle that must be broken: this cycle of denial in the hopes that things that you don't want to face will go away. To win that requires facing them head on, knowing that we can conquer any obstacle that comes. Let me stop talking about my mother here, but I will say this: She has to deal with that when she faces God. I'm not her judge nor am I coming back for her, but He is.

I'll be honest, Michael's death caused me to evaluate my life. Truthfully, it could've been avoided if he had received the love and support he needed. His death made me realize that I can't live my life being prissy or, as some would call it, having the "golden child syndrome."

I remember Michael was praying to God that he would save himself for marriage.

My baby daddy was only looking out for himself. Most of the men that I knew in High School, they had the attitude of "How can you say you love me?" And I fell right in that trap, much like Samson fell into Delilah's trap.

Speaking of praying, I must say this. We all know that life and death is in our tongue. Our actions play a significant role in this and this is really for those who attend a religious organization. I don't want to narrow it down to just one religion. We talk about abuse in the home, but we need to deal with it in religious organizations, too. Now, many will say that I'm wrong and I'll be willing to accept that. But think about our actions, we pretty much know if they are of God or not, unless we are deceived. How we treat people should be how God would treat people. Not everybody is going to take the time to dissect our hearts. We must be intentional in showing love to everybody. Everyone should be celebrated. Unfortunately, that is not the case. We can come up with any excuse in the book as to the why we don't, and then we have the audacity to tell people not to be offended if they're not celebrated. Just know that we are partial; it's sin, and depending on the severity, it's church abuse! No questions asked!

In closing, people need to address the holes in their hearts. We all make mistakes; we just have to own them and make amends as needed. If that means going to counseling, there's nothing wrong with that. We can't let anyone tell us there's something wrong with that. I wasn't abused, and I went. I'll be honest, I'm glad I went. If Carson were standing next to me, he, too, would say he was glad he went. One thing about counseling, though, is that you need to find the right counselor. Being abused in any form causes people to detach their thoughts from their emotions. It's important we connect our thoughts with our emotions, because it helps us understand our triggers so that we can overcome them. Michael and Genobia were unsuccessful in doing that because they both succumbed to suicide; however, Carson was successful. He had to stay with the process of counseling and not abort the process.

Just like Carson is leaving a legacy of triumph and overcoming, I want to leave that same legacy for my family. Despite the ill treatments, I am thriving and, like Carson, I desire to live the remainder of my life poured out for the service of others. Granted, if we all had that mindset, we can truly change the world and make a tremendous impact.

This is Stephanie Anderson, signing off. Good night, Diary!

AUTHOR'S NOTE

Dear Reader,

Carson's character and those that surround him in the story are a compilation of profiles based on research. As someone who has experienced abuse, my faith in Jesus Christ is everything. This is more important than anything else. It's not to say that I won't have struggles, but it can be dealt with better by having that assurance in Him. Without Him, I stand a greater risk of alcoholism, drug use and even suicide. Like so many who are fighting to live, I could've been Genobia and given up on my life, or I could've been vengeful and taken someone else's life due to the unresolved anger.

Some people won't understand the moods I go through when I am experiencing PTSD. If I didn't know Jesus, I would've given up, because I would've felt there's nothing else to live for. That doesn't mean that I don't battle with doubt, fears and concerns about my life. I am managing post-traumatic stress disorder (PTSD) and will overcome it. This is what happens when you've been abused for a period of time. Whether it is sexual, physical or emotional abuse, it affects your life.

I was also bullied during my first year in high school. It's a lot to handle, especially when you are a child or teenager, and it can take a toll as you try to catch up to your adulthood. I believe this is why some adults try to live out their childhood as an adult, and the world casts stones on them saying, "You're immature, you need to grow up."

As I wrote this novel, I thought about how many children and adults do rash things just to be heard. When we say that we're hurting, we look for someone to ask, "What's wrong?" Instead, however, finger pointing begins, and that is part of the problem. Clichés are dished out to the abused, because it makes us uncomfortable to get in the dirt and bear other people's burdens. I believe speaking words to those who've been hurt without providing a sounding board does not help them. Wounds caused by domestic abuse, emotional abuse, physical abuse, and sexual abuse don't heal overnight. Some who have been abused are embarrassed that they even need help. We want to run and hide, because something like that is happening in our world.

This story was partly written because I am concerned about the next generation. They're living in a world of bullying (physical, cyber, and AI), lack of parental support, dysfunction at home, bad grades, peer pressure, mental disorders, break-up of relationships, and loss of innocence. There are so many teenage boys and girls who fall victim to abuse, and they're trying to find a way out. We as a culture (church world and secular world) are punishing those who are abused, and this madness needs to stop.

If you've been abused, I pray that you found refuge in the midst of this story. I urge you, don't throw your life away. You might have identified with some of the characters, cried while reading this, and may still be trying to get through your trauma. Just so you know, male or female, it's okay to cry, and always know that God has a purpose for your life. Your life is precious! God loves you.

If you feel no human being is listening, God is listening. He heard my cries, and I have my life, and it's better now than I could have ever imagined! If God can do that for me, I know for a fact He'll do it for you. God sees all and knows all. God cares for you.

I know people can be cruel, and they will attempt to revictimize you. You're going to go through some harder things later in life (not to discourage you), but you need to know you have a lot to live for. God has placed in you multiple talents, and He's counting on you to fulfill them for His glory and to the world. Don't sit on your talents. Know that God's love is stronger than hate, hurt and abuse. He will help you.

Understand that the devil hates God's creation. In this case, we're talking about you, so, his objective is simply to steal, kill and destroy. And if you have suffered abuse, you may feel that your life/identity has been stolen, like you are destroyed and that your abuser should've killed you. Your abuser never loved you when he/she abused you, and there's a strong chance your abuser hates you more after the abuse. Your abuser is really tormented by the mere fact that you're still alive. You got out, and you made it out alive. Your abuser (used by the devil) may be trying to torment you by saying these phrases, "you're damaged goods, nobody wants you." Why are they doing that? Their souls are tormented and they are trying to pass it off on you; so, you can't fully heal and launch onto what God has planned for you. The devil has been a hater since day one, and he will be until he's thrown into the lake of fire. This is why your abusers, especially if they haven't repented, are being tormented. And they may think they're doing all right, even if they claim they are a leader of a church. Their respective church will believe his or her lies, but the truth is: they will suffer eternally if they don't repent. I'm very serious when I say that. Don't think their material wealth is a sign of approval. The scriptural reference for this is 2 Samuel 13:15-16 (KJV):

> ***15*** *Then Amnon hated her exceedingly; so that the hatred wherewith he hated her was greater than the love wherewith he had loved her. And Amnon said unto her, Arise, be gone.*
> ***16*** *And she said unto him, There is no cause: this evil in sending*

> *me away is greater than the other that thou didst unto me. But he would not hearken unto her.*

One thing I learned when I wrote the first Deaf, Dumb, Blind & Stupid book was that you don't say "get over it" to someone who's suffered long-term traumatic situations (and ended up with the disorders that I mentioned in the foreword), such as a woman who is suffering under the hand of domestic abuse, a child suffering under the hand of physical/sexual abuse, a hurt soul who's thinking and/or attempting suicide. We need the love of Christ, sympathy, empathy and understanding. To change the world, that's what's needed. In fact, it's recorded in James 1:19 to be slow to speak and swift to hear!

A friend of mine said to me that there are three things you should never tell a rape victim, and I wholeheartedly agree with this. Never say "It's your fault; you deserved it or you must have done something to cause it." Understand that rape is about power and control. You wouldn't act like "it's no big deal" if it happened to your mother, child, sister, brother, daughter, son, aunt, uncle, niece, nephew or yourself. Be mindful of making statements when something hasn't hit home for you, personally.

If you have allowed someone you love to be abused, and if you are in a position of power to stop it, end the silence and intervene to stop the abuse. I hope parents and adults will see the ramifications that can occur if you continue to neglect your child, students or those young people you mentor. Thank you for reading and taking heed to the message to fight for life.

Special Note:

I leave you with an essay that I wrote for Honestly Autism Day that took place April 16, 2016 at Timonium, Maryland. Typically, they just invite the winning essay to read at the event. Although my essay came in third place for the autistic adult category, the committee was impressed with my writing and the honesty of my essay that they wanted me to read it at the Express Yourself presentation at the event. The committee felt my essay spoke to what Honestly Autism Day is about.

When I was finished reading the essay at the event, I realized, after giving one of the panel members a hug, that the essay received a standing ovation. I acknowledged the applause, and then I proceeded out of the room to just go somewhere to be alone. With that said, here's the original essay:

At first glance, it would appear that my experience with autism has been negative. As a child, I was often ignored and even ostracized by my peers due to my lack of social skills. I was bullied by certain family members and fell victim to physical, sexual and verbal abuse. When my behavior plummeted, I was placed on Ritalin. The bullying continued. My parents didn't know how to work with me; since, they had never dealt with a child who wasn't normal. They tried to make me normal with discipline.

It. Didn't. Work.

My name is Tremayne Moore. For most of my life, I've lived with an untreated, unsupported case of High-Functioning Autism (formerly Aspergers). My disability diagnosis was buried so deep that I was able to enlist in the military. Yes, I'm a United States military veteran who has autism.

I first learned about autism in 2008 when celebrities were sounding the alarm. I didn't think anything of it until CNN did a documentary on autism. While observing the children's behaviors, I explained to my CPA exam study partner that I as a child I behaved the same way. This is when I asked my family about me being diagnosed with anything as a child. Of course I was given an emphatic no. So why was I medicated? Later that year, I learned that I had Post Traumatic Stress Disorder. Life experience plus being sexually abused did a number on me.

In 2014, I was tested and diagnosed with High-Functioning Autism. Knowing what was different about me gave me relief. I finally knew why I was in Special

Education during elementary school. My diagnosis gave me the peace of knowing that I was different and not broken. The special, positive things that have come from my experience with Autism is that knowing gave me the freedom to share my story to educate those around me who are oblivious to what autism really is. And, to raise awareness about how vulnerable children on the spectrum are to sexual abuse. Did you know that 1 out of 6 autistic children are sexually abused?

Having been rejected by family and peers as a result of my "special needs" has made me more compassionate. My conscience and my hurt won't allow me to knowingly hurt others. It gives me the courage to stand and to advocate for those who are unable to speak for themselves. Living with autism wasn't easy until I knew what I was up against. I hope that my words and my work encourage parents to seek help for their children as well as inspire those living on the spectrum to realize that even in their differences they are special and are needed to make the world a better place.

REFLECTIONS

Questions for Group or Individual Consideration

- Which character do you most identify with?
- What are some of the warning signs you see that Carson is being sexually abused?
- What other factors play a part in his abuse?
- How does mental disability make children an easier target for abusers?
- What is your group, congregation, or service club doing locally to bring awareness to abuse or suicide?
- What long-term effects are seen as a result of sexual abuse?
- How can you honor a person's truth while pointing them to proper counseling?
- In what ways do you feel religious organizations turn a blind eye to abuse?
- If you have children, how would you respond if your child came to you and said that someone you know was molesting them?
- How would you respond if your doctor/nurse informed you that your child has a mental disorder?
- Would you snoop on your child if he/she had a journal? And why?

- If you have children, are you doing your part in nurturing your child's gift? If you know someone who has a child, are you encouraging them to grow in their gift?
- What do you think was the message Carson was trying to convey with his life?
- Who do you identify best with in this story? And why?
- Why do you think parents take the side of the relative over the child when it comes to child physical and sexual abuse?
- Was Stephanie right or wrong for cutting off her mom?
- Should Stephanie forgive her mom for allowing Uncle Woody to abuse her son?
- Are you familiar with the phrase "what goes on in the house, stays in the house?" Do you still hold on to that mentality? And why?
- Why do you think abusers get a pass and the abused are revictimized through ridicule, shame and feeling like they are the outcast of the family?
- What were Carson's happy moments and what was therapeutic for him?
- Why do you think Carson was attracted to Jennifer?
- What kind of love did Genobia and Melissa need during their childhood?
- How would you respond to the death of Genobia?
- How would you respond to the social media post of Melissa?
- Would you suspect that Carson had a mental disorder during the course of this story? When did you notice it?
- How would you describe Dani's personality? Was Carson right or wrong for how he treated Dani?
- Did you keep a journal in your life? How beneficial was it to your life?
- Do you believe generation curses still happen today, and how do you stop the cycle?
- What does a generational habit look like in this story?
- Which character did you like? Which character did you despise?

TAKE THE LEAP!

Journal Challenge

Use this page as your opportunity to begin telling YOUR story.

See if you can fill in the prompts:

When I first began reading ______________________________

I felt like the character ______________________________

My growth looks like ______________________________

Reading this I recognize ______________________________

The parts of me that feel like I am regressing are

____

I was triggered by ______________________________

I think differently about

____

I am most disappointed by

____

I am most inspired by

____

I found ________________________________ intriguing.

I wish I had heard more about
______________________________________ in this book.

Moving forward, I am taking action to

____

RESOURCES

If you know a child who is going through one of the following:

1. Physical abuse
2. Sexual abuse/Rape
3. Bullying/Cyber-bullying
4. Depression
5. Suicide (contemplating/attempting)

Please contact and encourage the victim to contact the following:

National Suicide Prevention Lifeline
(800) 273-TALK (8255)
https://988helpline.org

Childhelp (Prevention and Treatment of Child Abuse)
(800) 4-A-CHILD, (800) 422-4453
www.childhelp.org

National Alliance of Mental Illness (NAMI)
(800) 950-NAMI (6264)

http://www.nami.org

National Domestic Violence Hotline
Assistance is available in English and Spanish with access to more than 170 languages through interpreter services. Help is available 24 hours, 365 days a year.
1-800-799-SAFE (7233) or TTY 1-800-787-3224
http://www.thehotline.org

Rape, Incest & Abuse National Network
(800) 656-HOPE (4673)
http://www.rainn.org/

ACKNOWLEDGMENTS

Wow, I'm amazed to be writing this sequel after 14 years of having released DDBS: Michael Anderson's Fight For Life (released May 2012). A lot of things have transpired between the time I released that book to this point in my life. The major thing is that I would lose my father five months after its release (September 2012). I'm grateful he was able to read the book; in fact, he chose the color scheme for the cover of that book. So, I desire to leave a little legacy of him in this book. The more I think about it, I debated within myself whether to take on this endeavor, considering how much I went through in my professional life and personal life while writing the first book. I will say that the responses from the first book were overwhelmingly positive, and I can't tell you how many times I cried in amazement after reading many reviews and for that, I'm truly grateful. With that said, it's time for the acknowledgments:

First and foremost, I thank my Lord & Savior Jesus Christ, for my testimony. In the words of a song that I love, I have scars, yet I'm still alive. Thank You for using this testimony to bless others, and my heart's desire is that people will see You through it all.

To my beautiful wife, Teleah, words can never say how much I love you. The first book would allow us to meet at an author event, and my life has never been the same since. You inspired this sequel, and this book took on a life of itself. I'm so grateful for the woman you are and all that He has in store for you. I guess you could say this is why I love you (smile). But seriously, not just in that, but in everything that you are. I love you with all of my heart.

To my immediate and extended family (also including my in-laws) – much love to you all.

I want to extend my sincerest gratitude to the following individuals (who have sown into my life):
Robert & Shantae Charles, you have been with me since day one of my writing career, and I'm grateful for all you've done for me.
Cynthia Portalatin, you already know I am grateful for our friendship. I thank you for carving time out of your busy schedule to proofread/copyedit this book.

I need to say this, because I know tomorrow is never promised. In the first book, I left some people anonymous, but I want it to be known publicly because of how much I value you: to Tracy Tennant and Dr. Lynn K. Wilder, I thank you for allowing me to pick your brains throughout both books and for contributing to the editing process. I appreciate you both tremendously.

I extend my appreciation and love to all the ministries, church families, public and private schools, organizations, bookstores, book clubs and different outlets that have supported my works. It's greatly appreciated.

To every author that I've met since the beginning of my writing career (circa 2009), I thank you and appreciate you. Thank you for sharing your wealth of knowledge with me, and I pray for much success in your writing career. I would try to name all of you, but let's be real, there are too many of you to name, so I'm just going to simply say thank you and I appreciate each of you greatly.

To those of you who have read the first book in this series, I'm very grateful for you. Many of you shared your stories with me, and they touched me greatly. And I would be less than a man if I didn't thank my fans who love and appreciate my other works. I'm grateful to God that I am able to minister to your soul and spirit.

The three special women that I mentioned (and left anonymous) in my first book that I wanted to thank, I want to now thank you publicly so that you know for certain who you are. You are: Monica Garrett, Leslie Anne (Coppin) Darcas, and Kimberly Brock. You could say I'm thanking you just because, and I want you to know that I have nothing but love for the three of you.

To all my friends (past, present and future), know that I love you and you're not forgotten. If I didn't mention you by name, charge it to my head and not my heart.

ABOUT THE AUTHOR

Tremayne Moore, founder of Maynetre Manuscripts, LLC, is an accountant, writer, psalmist, modern-day Griot, and Spoken Word motivational speaker. He is the author of the poetry series "You Can Take It" and the novel series "DDBS." Academically, he holds a Bachelor of Science Degree in Accounting from Florida Agricultural & Mechanical University and a Bachelor of Science Degree in Management Information Systems from Florida State University. Tremayne's life can be summarized with a quote from the Apostle Paul from Philippians: "Christ shall be magnified in my body; whether by life or by death."

For Publishing inquiries & speaking engagements:

Maynetre Manuscripts, LLC; Post Office Box 1819;
Owings Mills, MD 21117

Connect with Tremayne Online:
Website: www.maynetre.com
Blog: http://mayneman.blogspot.com
Email: tremayne_moore@yahoo.com

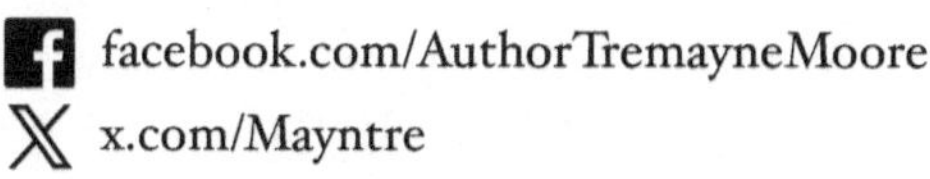

www.ingramcontent.com/pod-product-compliance
Lightning Source LLC
LaVergne TN
LVHW090609110826
845146LV00001B/314

* 9 7 9 8 9 9 0 8 0 7 3 6 5 *